JOHN ANDES

FARMER IN THE TAL

iUniverse, Inc.
Bloomington

Farmer in the Tal

iUniverse books may be ordered through booksellers or by contacting:

iUniverse
1663 Liberty Drive
Bloomington, IN 47403
www.iuniverse.com
1-800-Authors (1-800-288-4677)

ISBN: 978-1-4620-0763-9 (pbk)
ISBN: 978-1-4620-0764-6 (ebk)

Printed in the United States of America

iUniverse rev. date: 06/16/2011

Dedicated to Eugene Benton, Mary Estelle,
John Eugene and Mary Florence.

PREFACE

This is the farmer sowing the corn,
That kept the cock that crowed in the morn,
That waked the priest all shaven and shorn,
That married the man all tattered and torn,
That kissed the maiden all forlorn,
That milked the cow with the crumpled horn,
That tossed the dog,
That worried the cat,
That killed the rat,
That ate the malt,
That lay in the house that Jack built.

STORM

It starts. The low rumbling as if Nanna were moving furniture across the attic. Slow, low, and without order, the noises start in the northwest. They seem to be moving southeast. Their pace quickens ever so slightly as they approach Eden Valley. The pattern is renewed each late May. Farmers call the storms the late spring rains. Michael rolls over in his bed and searches the sky for the heart of the noises. There in the pitch, behind the clouds, the light roils like milk in Dad's coffee. The clouds are lit from behind. Their shape and density seem to change with each flash and splash of light. The lights form a broad band. They burst in a random manner. The entire canopy displays their advance. Gradual at first but quickening the closer it gets to the valley. The rumbling is now booming. With each flash, Michael counts…one thousand and one, one thousand and two, one thousand and three. At the beginning, he got to twelve. Now, the roar follows the light by six seconds. Is that six thousand yards or six miles? He asked Dad this more than once. Each time he forgets the answer. The lights are brighter. They overpower their cloud masks. The frequency seems to be one every five seconds somewhere in the sky. They are converging on the valley, just as they always do. The roars have changed mightily. Now the light is followed by the sound of renting fabric, which quickly becomes splintering wood and ends in a massive crack. As it splits the air, the thunder cascades from the sky down to earth, from the north to the south, as if each sound were an advancing column of soldiers sent to test an enemy.

With this sight and sound onslaught, there is precious little rain and air movement for now. The smell of electrified air is unmistakable. There is a cleanliness and purity to the night. The earth stands ready to receive. The count from light to crack is now one or less. The majestic thunderhead is poised. Two. Three. Four. Horrific jagged blasts of brilliance rain down on the dell within the valley as the storm pauses in its trek. Then the wind comes… from naught to gusts that bend the thick branches of the sycamores and oaks. The flashes continue for a minute. Maybe twenty or so. More than last time. There will be more next time. The cannonade is over. The storm doesn't move on, it simply stops and vanishes. Then the rain pours down. Sheets and sheets. The gray water is illuminated by the fast fading lightning. Streams will be gorged, ponds will over flow, and large foot-deep puddles will be created. The smell of sulfur kisses the night air. Michael thinks that Neen is right: *A big lightning storm is as close to God as you can get without dying.* Enervated, yet energized, Michael returns to sleep.

"Time to rise and shine. There's chores. No school, but lots of chores."

Mom's voice wafts as a harbinger. The smells of sausage and rolls warm the air in Michael's nose. The bathroom is a brief stop before clamoring down to the kitchen. Dad and Aaron are already inhaling sustenance in the dark of the early morning. Twyla Glee and Mom are waiting to sit after all the men have been served.

"Boys, did you hear that storm last night? It was a real snorter. After you take care of the milking, better check the fences. See if any sections were blown down by the wind. We need to scour the ground around the stream and pond for soft spots. Don't want any animals getting stuck or hurt. Then get the feed into the troughs and gas the tractors. We need to harrow the rows so the water don't stand and ruin the baby roots. Pass the jam."

"Michael, have you thought about what you want for your birthday?"

"No, Mom, I haven't given it much thought."

"That's a lie. He's been looking at the gun catalogs for weeks. Plus, he wants to get his driver's license. And a new fishing rod. The baby is greedy."

"Aaron, be still. This is Michael's sixteenth. And it's supposed to be more special. You remember your sixteenth don't you? You, your dad, and I took the train to Philadelphia. Twyla Glee and Michael stayed with your grandfather. We saw the sights. Went to a baseball game. Even stayed overnight in a big hotel. It was what you wanted. So, Michael can have what he wants. Michael, it's only a few days away. If we're going to make plans, we better start."

"Neen promised me one of his old rods. You know a three-sectioned bamboo. I've been thinking about my own 30.06 to go big game hunting next season with dad and his friends now that I'm sixteen. Aaron goes and he has his own gun. That's about it."

"Well, you think harder, son. You're my baby. After this birthday, I won't be able to say that in public."

"Becky, you're gonna sissify the boy if you keep treatin' him like a baby."

"Oh, Ruben, I am not. Let's talk about something else, now."

"No time. We got chores."

Like so many times before, Dad ended a conversation with Mom, as he wanted it ended, when he wanted it ended. The three men pushed away from the table and left through the back door.

"Twyla Glee, what do you think we should get Michael for his birthday?"

"I dunno, but, I'll ask Mary Ruth. Maybe she and Michael have spoken about something special he wants."

Michael thinks it's the same after each storm. The three men look for damage, but there is none. It seems the storms stay over the hill. The farm gets only the rain it needs. The ground will be muddy, so they get their heavy rubber knee-high boots from the mud room. Exiting the house through the side screen door three strangely gaited males plod to the barn and the chores of the morning.

"Aaron, you and Michael take the Deere and wagon up to the ridge and work your way along the fence. Take tools and wood to fix any breaks. I'll check the creek and pond to see if there's more work for you to finish this morning. Now get going. And don't go over to the other side."

The wagon is loaded with fence planks of several sizes, posts, a post hole digger, nails, hammers, wire, and cutters. There is no road up to the ridge, just a path. At the bottom, the path is visible, but seems to be swallowed up by the tall grass, weeds, and underbrush that comes down the hill. The hill is steep. The repair team must switch back four times to reach the fence. The fence is about two hundred feet from the top of the hill… and the beginning of other side.

Neen's great-grandfather had put the first fence at this point to keep out the animals that lived on the other side. The wild dogs or wolves would make

3

occasional forays over the top of the hill and raid the Hess farm. Chickens, sheep, even a calf or two in the spring would disappear. Sometimes the Hess's would find feathers or pelts, maybe bones on a chewed carcass as reminders of the unneighborly neighbors. Nighttime vigils were fruitless. Neen's grandfather said the dogs came when there was no moon. They were black as night and fast as the wind. Ever since the first fence, maintaining the protection has been vital. The sections are electrified between the posts. For more than six generations the Hess's have put hex signs on all the posts to ward off the evil from the other side.

As usual, the storm had done little damage to the barricade. As usual the other side had borne the brunt of the lightning and wind. The fence was nine feet tall and the planks between the posts were 2 x 8. No posts had to be replaced and only ten planks were broken. Most of them had rotted through and were pulled away by the wind. All sections and the electric wire had to be hand checked. A visual inspection was forbidden.

"I bet I know what Mary Ruth is going to do for your sweet sixteen."

"I don't know even if she is going to get me a present. So, if you know, don't tell me and ruin the surprise."

"I'll bet she's going to take you into the hayloft and take your cherry."

"That's nasty and unworthy of even a low life like you Aaron."

"She and I both know you've never been laid. And since I can't help you in that department, it's up to her."

"Let's drop the subject of my birthday, now."

"OK. But, you'd better be ready for the treat of your life, baby brother."

"Can you see Father?"

"Nah."

"Wanna go over the top and see what damage the storm did?"

"No."

"Why not?"

"Dad forbids it. And there is nothing there I would want to see."

"Forget Father for the moment. He can't see us and we can always say we had to do a lot of repair work. And, how do you know there is nothing there you want to see, if you've never been to the other side?"

"I've been plenty of times. I just don't want to go the morning after a storm."

"Why is that?"

4

"Because it's not right. Now let's get going back down to the farm."

"Coward."

"I'm not a coward. I've done more brave things than you have. I just don't want to do something foolish, for no reason, and for which I would get in trouble."

"OK. *Buauck. Buauck. Buauck.*"

"I am not a chicken. I'm wiser and braver than you, baby brother. Let's go."

The ride down the hill was absent of conversation.

"Fence all inspected and mended?"

"Yes sir."

"Good, I found a few holes near the creek. Take some earth from behind the barn and fill them in. Even two teenage boys can find the spots I mean. When you're done, it'll be lunchtime. You can do the barn chores after that."

They had lunch outside at the big table under the oak.

Barn chores are the worst. Inside, with little ventilation in the heat of the day. Dirt and feed dust covers a sweaty body and clogs a nose. The good side of barn chores in the afternoon is that a splash in the creek is permitted when they are done. A little swimming hole had been created by damming up the creek and digging out the bed behind the stone barrier. Water escaped through the gaps in the rocks, but enough rushing water remained to form a pond two feet deep. In late May and early June, the water is still cold from the winter months, so splashing for refreshment and cleaning is not a long-term event. Just take off the work boots, pants, and shirt and wade in. Soap provides a reason to be active. Rinse clean. Dry in the sun during the walk to the house.

Dinner, as always, was fit for the king and his court.

"If you want, I can make you a special dinner for your birthday, Michael. What would you like?"

"You know my favorite. Lamb chops, succotash, fried potatoes, and sliced tomatoes with your special dressing."

"You are so predictable it's boring."

"Hush, Aaron. If that's what he wants for his birthday dinner, then that's what he shall have."

"I'll make some strawberry ice cream for the dinner."

5

"Twyla Glee, that's very thoughtful. Maybe we should have a picnic party. I can invite Mary Ruth. Would you like that, Michael?"

"Yes ma'am that would be nice."

"How about we invite your friend, Sarah Miller, Aaron?"

"But, it's not a date. She's just coming over because it's a party for baby Michael."

"As you wish. You don't have to be harsh about it. Are you embarrassed that we see you with her? If so, I won't invite her. But, I must say most of my friends have seen you two together. I think its time your father and I get a chance to meet Sarah. There's no sense in keeping your feelings under a basket."

"It's not that. It's just that we've been having some tough times lately. Sarah is talking about leaving the county and moving to Philly. I'm not ready to make any kind of commitment, but if she leaves, she leaves. And, I don't want her to leave."

"Well maybe a family party will help her decide to stay."

"What about me? Can I have a friend over?"

"I thought I'd invite Mr. Landis from town. You know the polite young man who drives the delivery truck for the mill."

"Mom that would be special. He is nice."

"Twyla's got a boy friend. Twyla's got a sweetheart."

"No I don't."

"Twyla and Elmer sitting in a tree. K-I-S-S-I-N-G. First comes love, then comes marriage, then comes Twyla with a baby carriage."

"Stop. Mommy, make Aaron stop."

"Hush, Aaron. Stop teasing Twyla. It hurts her."

Twyla pushes away from the table and runs upstairs. The slam of her bedroom door is followed by whimpering, barely audible at the table.

"Now march upstairs and make peace with your sister."

"Ah, Dad."

"Ah nothing. Do as I said. You know how fragile she is. Now march and apologize. And it better be good. I'm going to ask her later tonight."

"Father, may I be excused. I have a few odds and ends I need to take care of in the barn."

"After you and Aaron help your mother clear the table."

"Why must I do Twyla Glee's chore?"

"Because I told you to. Every once in a while it's nice to give her a break from her chores."

"She never gives me a break. She never helps in the barn or out in the field."

"Michael, you and I know she's special and needs special care sometimes. This is one of those times. So, think of her needs now."

"OK."

"Clearing the table takes ten minutes. Aaron can do his part when he returns from apologizing for being an ass."

"I'm going to the barn, then over to Jimmy Hauck's for an hour. I'll be back before it gets too dark."

Through the barn. Out the back door and sprint across the field to the hill. Keeping low makes running difficult. The path to the fence is protected from sight by weeds on both sides. There are two planks that are loose and can be pushed aside to create an opening. Michael squeezes through and struggles in the dense bushes and vines to the top of the hill. There is plenty of light to see the forbidding monolith in the center of the clearing in the Tal.

This is the forbidden land; an evil place. For centuries, the Hess family and neighbors have known of the Tal and the building in it. They have tried to protect themselves from the evil with fences, but most of all they work very hard to ignore it. They know bad things come from the Tal. Some people say wolves. Some say bears. Some whisper about evil spirits. Over the ages there are stories of men in hunting parties who went into the Tal. Some were injured. Some died. And, in some cases calamity befell them and their families after the visit. This led many to say the Tal was cursed. For them that was enough. No one went there. They hoped by not having contact with or thoughts about the Tal and the building, the evil would not harm them. The people behaved like little children who believe there are demons under their beds. But, Michael is smarter than that. He knows the Tal is just another piece of land. And the building is nothing more than an abandoned house. There is no evil. There is only superstition.

There is no trail to the bottom of the hill and without his knife to cut away the foliage, the trip is difficult. It takes about fifteen minutes to reach the floor. Then he sees them. Small craters burnt and blown in the earth by last night's lightning. There are eight around the big building and four near the crab apple tree. The biggest, ugliest crab apple tree in the county. Neen said it had been a chapel, but no one had ever been inside to confirm this. It looked more like a castle of ancient Europe. Like the ones in Michael's history book at school. The first crater measures about eighteen inches deep and two feet across. Nothing but the gray ashes of burned earth and undergrowth. The second and third, the same. The fourth crater is much larger… about three feet deep and six feet across. In the fading light, stones are visible. Three black, gnarled circles and two semi circles. These would make wonderful additions to Michael's collection. He scoops them up and puts them in his pocket. Suddenly, the breeze and rustling of the branches threatens. Is it just the leaves or is it the sound of another visitor shuffling in Naast Tal? Time to head for home. The night's raiding party is being scared off. The struggle up the hill is more difficult. As if there is a force tugging on Michael, trying to keep him on the other side. Michael slips out of his boots and hides them in a special place in the barn, not the mud room. He enters the house through the kitchen door. His father is sitting at the kitchen table leafing through a stack of magazines, he never reads.

"Father, Jimmy Hauck stopped by the other day."

"How is Jimmy?"

"He's great. This summer, he got a job at the factory, cleaning out the boxcars that bring the raw materials to make the linoleum. He works the graveyard shift from 11 to 7. Works Sunday night through Thursday night. No work Friday or Saturday. We talked about going to the shore some weekend, if it's OK with you, I mean. We'd leave Friday morning and get back early Sunday night. I'd work extra hard the week before and get all the chores done by Thursday night. Waddya think?"

"Your mother and I will discuss it, but I don't see any problems. Except how would you get there?"

"Jimmy said he could borrow his brother's car since he can't use it now that he is in jail. Jimmy's been driving for about a year with his license and everything."

"We'll talk tomorrow. Now it's bedtime. We have a full day tomorrow. You'll need your rest. Sleep well."

"Thanks, Father. See you in the morning."

On the top shelf above Michael's bed is a wooden box in which Michael keeps his special stuff. Pictures of his family and a picture of Mary Ruth Martin in her high school cheerleading outfit, an Eagle feather, his pen knife and the fishing knife Neen gave him when he was twelve, a cross made from two rusted cut nails and a piece of copper wire, and his rock collection. Michael had been collecting rocks or stones for years. He has about thirty of every color. Black with white stripes, red with dark blue speckles, and granite chunks of tan and pink. None of them bigger than the palm of his hand and most the size of a quarter. For his science project, he wrote about the rocks. All but three are indigenous to this part of the country, although two are rare, because they are normally found in deep excavations like mining. The three that his teacher could not identify from any source book in the public library were sent to State College. They came back with a letter explaining that their laboratory was not equipped to perform the necessary analysis, but they looked like shards of a meteorite or some other extraterrestrial body. That's all.

Now the five new ones. Black. No hint of any color. He knows that pure black is the fusion of all colors until there is no differentiation or hue. And the semi-circles seem to have been torn from something. They are twisted as if they had been partially melted and cooled in their contorted form. There are tiny blisters on the surface of the circles as if the heat was recent and age had not yet smoothed over the heat's assault. Michael notices that the new stones do not reflect light. They seem to absorb it. And they are cool. Even when he squeezes one or two in his hand for thirty seconds, the stones are cool to the touch. Next year he'll go to State College with Neen and ask the Geology professor about the rocks. Neen went to college there. Maybe they'll pay more attention to a grad.

Michael will go to college, like all the men in his family. He has earned all A's at school. He has been tested and they said he had a very high IQ. He scored at the top of the standard tests used to determine college eligibility. They made it possible for him to take a history of religion course at the local community college this spring. Next fall, he will take another religion course and then maybe a philosophy course in the spring. Michael is gifted and everybody wants to expand his mind and fill it with knowledge. He feels more comfortable talking with adults than he does talking to his classmates.

Another night in early June brings another storm. The chores take their toll and Michael sleeps through the night.

SWARM

The cows are waiting by the large double doors. They know it's milking time. Michael opens the doors and the herd plods to slots in against the walls. They don't rush or fight to get to a station, because they know which is theirs. But, their size in the limited space of the barn's floor causes them to bump into each other like good-natured people who go to big sporting events.

"How many head are ready at their stations?"

"All of them."

"Cut it out. I'm serious. Count them."

"OK. Why?"

"I think we're missing one."

Michael goes back inside the barn and counts.

"You're right; there are only sixty-five ready for milking. One is still out in the field. A straggler. Probably an older one. Just tired."

"I looked outside and didn't see any motion."

"It's not yet light. You couldn't see your hand if it weren't attached."

"I'll hook them up, while you go out and find the lost one."

Michael heads out through the yard and over the mess deposited by the early morning crowd. The sun's glow begins to warm the sky to his left. Shadows and shapes take the place of pitch. Past the barnyard and out to the field, where the Guernseys graze and sleep after their milking, there is nothing in sight. He turns his stare to the creek. Often they splash across to get newer grass or to find shade in the summer. Now the sun is shooting slivers of white gold over the hill and chasing the darkness for the day. Michael dances across the natural stone walkway in the creek splashing only a little water on his boots. He scans the field before the hill, and swats a black fly on his arm.

The humming of the milking machines is faint. He has never listened to it from this distance. There is no motion and no cow under the trees asleep. Michael walks toward the sun and the rocks. They never go there, but maybe last night's storm scared one to do something dumb. That's a laugh. Dumb cow is redundant. Seeing nothing on the rocks, he heads toward the slope to the hill. Now he can survey all the details of the pasture. It is day. The tufts of onion grass are damp and the occasional rock beneath his step is slippery. The bugs begin to crawl, hop, and fly. He swats another black fly. Then two more hover near his eyes. He shoos them away. The humming is getting louder. It's not humming it's buzzing. About midway between the base of the hill and the fence is a huge swarm of all manner of insects. It looks like mostly black flies.

The swarm is about twenty feet above the fence height and maybe thirty or thirty-five feet long. It looks like a huge black blanket floating in the air, contorting and twisting. Parts of it pull away from the main body and dive into the grass. The diving formation is wedge-shaped and six feet wide. The changing shapes swoop down into the tall weeds and reappear twenty seconds later to meld back into the main group. Then another form dives and returns. Then another and another. All the while the basic swarm is hovering and growing with late arrivals, who were probably feasting on cow dung still warm from last night. Climbing the hill to about thirty yards from the swirling, diving mass, Michael sees its reason for being: the partially devoured carcass of a cow.

His heart rushes to maximum overload and he turns to the barn.

"Aaron. Aaron. Come quick! You got to see this. It's terrible."

He stumbles as he runs down the hill. He bumps into a bush and slides on a rock. The falling does not stop his headlong rush from the sight and to the safety of his brother. He rolls, slams his arms and knees on the ground, rights himself and keeps on. Now his shirt and pants are dirty and grass stained. Mom will wonder.

"Aaron. Aaron. Come here. I found the lost Guernsey."

His breath is depleted as Aaron emerges from the barn.

"Where?"

"Up on the hill about half way. You got to see it."

11

Aaron is now trotting to the creek. He crosses and both boys head back up the hill.

"Good God almighty, look at those flies. There must be a million of them in the swarm. It looks like a solid mass. And they're diving like they're attacking something."

"They're eating the dead cow. We gotta go up there and get rid of the carcass so it doesn't attract other vermin."

"Stay here, I'll get Dad. He'll know how to get rid of the flies."

Aaron's retreat is faster than Michael's approach. In ten minutes, his older brother and Dad are coming out of the tractor shed with the Deere and the flatbed loaded with equipment and a large tarp. Michael jumps on the flatbed. Dad navigates the tractor to within fifty feet of the revolving, gyrating mass of gray-black filth and disease. He takes his .410 Remington shotgun from under the tarp and grabs two fists' full of shells.

"This is what's going to happen. I'm going to fire blasts into the swarm. The blasts of birdshot will kill some and drive the others crazy with the rush of air. You boys are going to run over to the carcass and pour gasoline over it. Then light it and get away fast. That's how we'll get rid of the mess. But, before all that, we need to build a firebreak about fifteen feet from the carcass. Each of you take a shovel and be prepared to turn the earth in a path about six to eight feet wide as I drive the tractor in a circle around the carcass. Hurry. The longer we wait, the more infested the flies get and the more likely they can spread disease to the others in the herd."

The tractor and wagon make a circle to flatten weeds in a space wider than the weeds are tall. The circle is dangerously close to the flies. They make forays from the feast to the machine and wagon, the driver and the two boys turning the earth behind the wagon. Swatting and shooing disturb the earth turning. The boys have pulled their t-shirts from under their work shirts and over their heads. The sleeves are pulled over the hands and buttoned at the fingertips. Dad looks like a beekeeper as he joins in. He is ahead of them with a pickaxe swinging mightily, chewing up huge chunks of sod, green, and roots. He swings to the right, the center and then to the left as he almost runs. The boys struggle to keep pace.

"OK, boys, now is the time of our deliverance."

The first blasts punch holes in the swarm like holes in smoke. The holes are filled immediately. The second round of blasts follows shortly thereafter.

The holes fill less quickly. Two more explosions are followed by two more. The tiny birdshot must be killing some flies, because there are so many of them so close.

"We're going to need more than this first attack. Now take the gas cans and be ready. Remember stay low to the ground. The bird shot spreads quickly. I don't want to hit either one of you."

The boys stand at attention as four more shots ring in their ears and echo through the valley. The black monolithic mass disperses then quickly reforms.

"Now. Go fast. Don't let the flies bite you. They're very angry now and they'll attack for sure."

Michael pushes through the weeds and opens the five-gallon can. As he is about to pour, his eyes snapshot the dead animal. Head open above the eyes. Throat slashed. The gash is about six inches wide and a foot and a half long. Belly torn open. Ribs exposed. The animal is empty. Heart and other vital organs missing. Shanks and shoulders intact. What could have done this? Wolves? Bears? Men? They pour, swat, and shoo. He pours the gasoline over the remains of the top half, while Aaron does the same over the bottom half. The pestilence carriers do not go far away from the carrion. Michael feels two bites. He squashes the culprits instantly. His can drops. Aaron scowls. Cans empty, they both step back three feet. The gasoline will protect the beast from further attack only temporarily. Some flies must find a new food source. Michael holds the rolled paper. Aaron strikes a match. It breaks.

"Hurry boys, your friends are re-grouping for an attack. They want their breakfast."

The second match breaks. Michael grabs the box and strikes three at once. The flame licks the paper roll, which is turned twice to ensure a complete light. Michael throws the torch. Aaron has already run back to Dad.

The ignition is an explosion as the fireball instantly expands six feet wide and rises rapidly above the weeds... above the fence height. The black smoke surrounds the ball and plumes outward and into the clear morning sky. The flames that chase the smoke are red, brown, and yellow.

"Aaron, take the tractor back to the farm and hook up the water wagon. We need to be sure this fire can't spread. Hurry."

The fire fueled by the flesh, hide, bones, and flies snaps and crackles more loudly than any Yule Log Michael ever heard. The normal breeze on the hill becomes a frenzied sirocco whipped by the flames. The acrid stench of cowhide and hair permeates Michael's eyes and nose causing tears and mucus to flow profusely. The assault on his senses is not constant, but wavers with the wind. Temporary relief is followed by long moments of irritation. Holding shovels, the two circle the pyre. Safe from the swarm, which was either devoured or driven off by the infernal explosion, the man and boy are left to swat sparks and small flames. Aaron's return signals the next phase. As Aaron slowly drives the tractor around the firebreak, Michael lets water flood from the rear of the wagon creating a circular marsh.

"Michael, I want you to stay here until the fire is out. Make sure the flames don't leap the break. Aaron will fill a couple of buckets for any emergencies. When the flames die down, let us know and we'll come back and help bury the ashes. In the meantime, you can begin digging the grave. My guess is that the fire should be out in an hour at the most. If anything goes wrong just holler. I'll be lookin' up at you from time to time."

It's only right. Michael left the fence open last night and the animals from the Tal must have gotten through at that spot and attacked the cow. But, the opening was down at the other end of the property and the cows rarely cross the creek at night. The wolves or bears must have purposefully gone hunting for the Guernsey, killed it, and dragged it up the hill to eat. Why didn't they eat it where they killed it? That would be natural. There were no signs of a scuffle near the creek. There were no drag marks up the hill. And the cow would have left marks. So, it had to be killed up here. But, Michael had never seen a cow on the hill either in day or night. There is nothing of interest for them up here. The burial pit must be six by three by four to hold all the bones and the ashes. If the cow didn't wander up here, it was led up here. That requires a human. But, who would do that to one of the Hess cows? Jimmy Hauck might know of someone who would think killin' a cow was a funny trick. Maybe it was Gene Dracal. Michael ever liked that snot bag. Always sayin' he was too good for the farmer. Maybe it was Joe Killian. He is a mean prankster. He set a cat on fire one Halloween. Jimmy will know for sure. Shoveling in the heat of the sun and the fire is brutal. The reek of the fire adds to the discomfort. Waves of nausea begin low and slow, but they build quickly. Finally, relief. The vomit projectiles into the pit. Smaller after loads are spit out like lumps of snot. Michael's eyes are pouring and his entire body is cool and sweating, just like a fever. When the heaving is over, he has to sit to catch his breath.

"Are you done, baby brother? What's that mess? Did you play throw-up? Was the work too much for da baby?"

"Shut up and leave me alone."

"Dad will be here soon and the body vault better be ready."

"It's ready. Why don't you check the bar-b-q and see if it's ready for the pit? If you're not too scared."

"I'm not scared. I checked. It's almost ready. Maybe if we pour the water on the embers, we can bury the carcass before Dad comes back. That'll make it look like you did a good job right before your birthday, too."

The plume of the fetid-smelling steam causes Aaron to wretch. Michael smiles. Using their shovels, they push the ashes and charred remains to the pit. Then they shovel up about six inches of earth where the pyre had been. This they dump on the remains of the animal. They cover all with the tarp and plop rocks around the edge. Then, the brothers shovel dirt onto the pit, jump on the mound and fill in the dents more to be sure all is safe. Last, they pour the remains from the gas cans on the earth works to obliterate any remnant odor, which might attract the wolves or bears.

"Boys, that'll do. I think we'll be safe from the fire spreading or the animals coming back. Now, I want you to go over the fence, plank by plank, to be absolutely sure there are no gaps or holes for the animals to get through. Be sure you check the wire for breakage. An alarm would have gone off if the animals broke the wire. And, for Neen's sake check all the hex signs. He'll ask me if we did. So do. Now scoot. There's a lot more to do when you're done with the fence."

"Aaron, I'll start at the west. You start at the east. We'll meet back here. I'll race ya'."

"Boys, this is not a race. Be thorough. We can't afford to have the animals from the other side think of this as their cafeteria."

At each end of the fence is a huge stone wall that marks the beginning of the Tal. The copper wire, which runs from post to post, is electrified and hooked up to an alarm in the barn. If there had been a break, the bell would have sounded and the light would have turned on. The dogs would have gone crazy with barkin' and howlin' and the family would have heard and seen the alarm and responded with guns at the ready. There are three six-inch diameter hex signs on each post. The circle on top contains a gold star cascading white light downward onto a dark blue and green mottled field. On the middle circle are two roses, one blood red rose and one white, as well as a dark brown cross on a flesh tone background. The third circle is a swirl of colors and soft patterns emanating from the center and flashing to the rim.

The hex signs are a carry over from centuries ago, designed to ward off evil and to bring good luck. Neen believes they keep the farm safe. He had the circles created and prayed over by Amos Zug, pastor of the oldest congregation in the county. Pastor Zug espouses the use of hex as signs of true faith. They are made with pure elements, their messages are scripture based, and the shapes are as perfect as man can make them. Ruben does not believe in the power of the hex, but he will say nothing to offend or disrespect his father. Neen had the hex signs made from designs in the old bible. The bible sits in a glass case in parlor, a place of honor for the special book. Neen says the bible is witness to all things spiritual and temporal. The last pages in the tome contain a record of the family since before there were cars, electricity, or governments. The entries cover major events for the family and for the county: wars, epidemics, storms, and the like. The book's twelve-by-eighteen inch wooden and leather cover is held by brass hinges and a large clasp. The bible is written in old German. Neen can read it easily. Dad has a little difficulty. Michael is learning. The first entry in the back of the bible is dated July 1706.

Michael walks along the fence sections pushing and pulling on the planks to be sure they are secure. After eight sections there are no loose planks or broken wire. All the hex signs are in order on the posts. Section nine is where he entered the Tal. The two planks near the west post are loose. He must have forgotten to reattach them when he escaped the darkness with his stones. This must have been where the animals entered the Hess farm. The planks are secured to the top runner. The copper wire is unbroken. How did the wolves get through the hole between the planks without tripping the wire? Then Michael notices one post. Then, the other. Both posts are missing the middle hex; the discs are lying facedown on the ground. As he goes to re-nail the signs, Michael notices that each is slightly out of perfect circular shape due to indentations. A large wolf or bear could have stepped on the metal sign and bent it with his weight, while the claws scratched the metal. That couldn't happen to both signs. Only a human could do that. It matters not;

they are back in their desired place. The remaining planks, wire, and hexes are checked and found to be in order.

"Michael, did you find anything?"

"Just two loose planks. I nailed them secure. And you?"

"Nothing. Let's get down to the house. I'm hungry."

Lunch is taken in silence. Dad is disappointed. Aaron told him about the two planks. Michael could feel the anger. The loss of the cow is his responsibility.

"Aaron I need you to go to the mill store and buy enough feed for next month. Breakfast for the herd and two types of feed for the chickens…pullets and layers. And see if Mister Mummaw has any more copper wire. I think we should add a second line to the fence. We'll need about two thousand feet. And we'll need a lot more of the glass condensers… the kind we can nail to the posts. We'll run the second line through the same box; it's got two sets of terminals. Becky is there anything you need from the store?"

"Yes, a ten-gallon galvanized tub and a case each of one-quart and two-quart jars for canning. Plus, a case of paraffin wax blocks. The fruits and vegetables will be comin' in soon."

"How about you, Twyla Glee?"

"Nothing special, Daddy. I would like to go along if it's all right with you and Mommy."

"I don't see why not. Michael, Aaron will need your help loadin' the truck. So, you'll go too. I'll give you a check to pay for the supplies. Can you be responsible for that?"

"Yes sir."

"That'll leave you and me all alone, Becky. Do you think we can manage?"

His grin complements her blushing.

Aaron drives the Ford 350 like he owns the world. He roars down the lane. If it were covered with black top, it would be a long driveway. The tires screech as he shifts into third on Hunsecker Mill Road. The three bodies slide on the front seat. Twyla likes the fair-ride like action. She rarely smiles. Now she is giggling. The trip to the Hunsecker Mill takes Aaron twenty minutes. All the time, the radio is locked on WRBL "Rebel Music…The Sound Your Parents Hate". The volume is as painful as the music. This is Aaron's pleasure of the world to make this chore less than painful.

The store is four stories of every imaginable item for the day-to-day living on a farm. Michael's social science teacher describes it as an early twentieth century deep country Wal-Mart. The first floor is crammed with items for the house, women's and children's clothes and a lot for the kitchen and bathroom. Stuff that interests wives and mothers. The second floor is more for men… clothes, guns, and tools for fixin' things. The third floor has hard to find things, like parts for washers, dryers, refrigerators, and freezers. The basement contains repair material like boards, kegs of nails, wire, fencing items and the like. Only Mister Mummaw and his boys know where everything is. Prices and inventory are kept in a big book by the cash register. Receipts are written in pencil on a large pad with carbon paper.

"Watcha' lookin' for, Michael? Are you gonna' take up kitchen work?"

"Jimmy, Nah, my mom needs the jars and paraffin. I'm glad you're here. I need to ask you something."

"What?"

"Today we found one of the Guernseys slaughtered up on the hill. It could have been the work of wolves or it could have been the work of some kid who thinks it's neat to be evil."

"I know, you're thinkin' about Joe Killian. It couldn't have been him. He's out of town. I think his folks sent him to spend the summer with his uncle over in Berks County. You know Mr. Killian's brother, the one who runs a big farm… about ten times larger than yours? He needs a lot of help, so he pays kids to work the farm. Besides it gets Joe out of the house to a place where he can't cause problems for Mr. and Mrs. Killian. They're getting too old to deal with his antics. It couldn't have been him, 'cause he left the day school let out."

"What about Gene Dracal?"

"He and his pals are always lookin' down their noses at us. They got too much time on their hands. None of them work. They all got cars and they're mean."

"Do you think they would be so mean as to kill one of our cows?"

"I wouldn't put anything past that stuck up bastard."

"The cow's neck was slashed. A broad, deep, and long gash. The belly was cut open and all its organs were removed."

"Sounds like Gene and his buddies are trying to scare you. Make it look like wolves or something else from over the hill. If it was Gene, I doubt if you'll ever prove it. I doubt if he'll come back. He's smart enough to know your dad would keep a close watch on the herd after one loss."

"Yeah, I guess you're right. Hey, I spoke to my father about us goin' to the shore. It looks pretty good. I'll need two weeks' notice so I can get all the chores done before the weekend. When were you thinking?"

"The fourth is on a Thursday. That means I don't work Thursday night. We could leave Wednesday morning around eight and have five full days at the shore. Five days of sun, women, and beer."

"That's a lot of time away from the farm, but I think I can work on Father."

"That's great. See ya later."

"Twyla, are you about done? Did you want to buy anything for yourself? I've got what Mom wants. I'll go out to the loading platform and check on Aaron so I can pay for everything at once. I'll be right back."

Of all the people Michael knows, Twyla Glee is the most deserving of attention. She is kind. Her needs are basic. Her mind is a little slow, but her heart is good.

"Aaron, are you ready?"

"I was born ready."

His bravado is boring. The truck bed is packed and the rear shocks reflect the load. There will be room for the coils of wire on top of the feed. The items for Mom will fit behind the bench seat.

"Bring the truck to the front door and I'll load what I bought. Do you have the receipt?"

"Yes. While you're loading women's stuff, I'm going to get a soda. Want one?"

"Sure and get one for Twyla."

Wire, condensers, tub, jars and paraffin loaded.

"Aaron got us both sodas. The truck is loaded. We're ready to go home. Are you ready?"

More ear splitting cacophony for the ride home.

NEEN

Requiring the two boys to unload and stack the bags of feed in the hot sun and after the labors of the morning, is Ruben's way of letting Michael know that he knows who is responsible for the cow's death. There is no real proof, just the father's almighty judgement. The dust that filters through the burlap bags covers the boys, cakes the insides of their noses, and slides into their lungs. The coughing and spitting is testimony to the invasiveness of the fine particles.

"Michael. Aaron. Could you use some help?"

"We can always use help with hard work, Neen. Father set us about this chore, and I believe he wants us to complete it by ourselves."

Neen is the grandfather. Isaac Abraham Hess lives in the little house on the other side of the barn. Originally built for parents eight generations ago, the single floor dwelling is his alone. Nanna, his wife of over fifty years, died ten years ago. She caught the flu and died in her sleep two days later. She's buried in the family cemetery at the property's west end.

"I'm sure your father won't mind my pitching in. Sort of earning my keep. Here's what we'll do. Aaron, you unload onto the wheelbarrow. I'll wheel it into the barn. Michael, you unload and stack. It'll sure beat you carryin' the bags by twos on your shoulders. Everybody does a little so no one does too much."

The assembly line starts. Neen is bony, short, and slightly bent from years of labor on his farm. In his younger days he was wiry. The farm is his. Ruben may run it and be responsible for it, but as long as Neen is alive, the farm is his.

People throughout the county call it Isaac Hess's place. And, they don't mean the little house. Although gnarled from arthritis and the occasional break, Neen's hands are gentle. He can caress a bird or a baby. Honest and true to his family and the farm, he shows respect to all he meets. Respect garnered from working the land; working in concert with something greater than he. Grandfather is incredibly strong. Michael has seen him lift a bale of early cut hay in each hand and toss them over his head to the loft. He never raises his voice except to laugh. There are stories of his strength of will and purpose. When he came back from college, he took the job of schoolteacher in the one-room schoolhouse in the next valley. The job was necessary to supplement the farm's income…depressed by the war. The first day, the older kids were testing him with disrespect and rowdiness. At lunch, an eighth grader, Jake Hostetter, challenged Neen to a fight. Jake outweighed Neen by sixty pounds and stood over him by four inches. He should have been out of eight grade three years before, but he was real slow and real mean. Neen knew that if he backed down or lost, he would never be taken seriously and no student would learn from him. The fight lasted exactly three punches. Jake went down and didn't get up until Neen extended his hand and helped him. Nothing was ever said about the fight, except Jake's folks sent the new schoolteacher a ham, some flour, and a basket of vegetables two days later. Neen said: *The farmer has to show the bull who runs the farm.*

"Aaron, what's wrong?"

"Neen, my left hand itches so much. And it's beginning to swell and hurt."

"Let me see."

"Son, you've been bitten by something. Bitten fierce a few places. We need to tend to the bites. Do you remember being bitten?"

"The flies. The black flies around the carcass."

"What carcass?"

"The cow that was slaughtered up on the hill. We had to burn it and bury it. About a million flies were feeding on the remains that the wolves left. When Michael and me went to pour gasoline on the carcass, a few flies got on my hand. I felt the bites, but didn't think much of it."

"We have to think about it now. Let's get you to the house. Now."

Michael followed the older man as he walked beside Aaron to the house.

"Becky, Aaron needs our immediate attention. I'll take him to his bedroom and make sure he gets undressed. You make a paste: one part water, two parts flour, and three parts salt. Add more salt if necessary to thicken it. Make about two cups for now. Where's Ruben?"

"He's downstairs in the shop. Hadn't we better call Doctor Hoffman or take him to the Emergency Room at the hospital?"

"Becky, there is no time for those niceties. You can call the doctor once we have started the treatment. Michael, get your father up here, I need him."

The boy scampers. Within seconds the entire family is in the kitchen.

"Ruben, go to my house and get the small leather bag from the cabinet in the bathroom. Take the brown bottle from the bag and bring it to the kitchen. Then I want you to make a drink for Aaron. Two tablespoons of the powder from the bottle, four tablespoons of linseed oil, and eight ounces of milk. Stir it until the entire drink is a deep red brown color. You may need to add a touch more powder. Then bring it to me."

"Michael, I'll need your belt for a tourniquet, and get a big bucket."

"Twyla Glee, we're gonna need a lot of towels and a basin. Now, everybody, about your tasks, Aaron needs our help."

Neen is holding Aaron by this time. Pale and sweating profusely, the boy begins to slump on the old man. Even for Isaac, it's not easy hauling the boy up the stairs. Michael follows belt in hand. Aaron is stripped of his external dignity and placed under the sheet with his left arm hanging over the side.

"Got to keep the poison from getting to the brain or the heart. Slow down its path through the body. Put the tourniquet above the bicep, Michael, and make sure it's real tight. Aaron needs you to help him; he can take the discomfort of the belt."

"Becky, hand me that paste. Good, it's starting to stiffen."

The old man slathers the paste over Aaron's hand and wrist, making sure to daub extra exactly where Aaron had been bitten. Ruben enters the room with a large tumbler. Neen moves the big bucket below Aaron's head.

"Now, son, I'm gonna' give you something to drink. It won't taste very good, but it will do you good. You got to drink it all in one sitting. No seconds. You'll have to sit up for a moment then you can lie back down. Do you understand?"

The patient barely nods, but somehow pulls himself to a sitting position.

Neen holds the tumbler and Aaron gulps reflexively. Ten giant swallows and the potion is gone. Aaron slumps back to the sheets.

"Twyla Glee, fill the basin with very cold water and be ready to put compresses on Aaron's head, neck and chest. Can you get some ice for the basin to keep the water cold?"

"Yes, Grandpa. I'll be right back."

"Becky, you can call Doctor Hoffman now if you want. There will be no need for the hospital."

Mother disappears downstairs.

"Ruben, go to the parlor and get the bible for me, will you please. Also, make me another glass of the medicine."

Ruben disappears downstairs.

"Michael, Aaron has been poisoned. We must be diligent and true to prevent further harm to the boy. In all this fuss, I never asked if you were bitten by the flies."

"They tried. A couple of nips, but I was able to shoo them away before they did too much damage. Here, look at my hands. There are four little pinpricks. No itch, pain, or swelling. I guess I was lucky."

"Yes, I guess you were."

The old man stares through the window to the sky and the hill.

"Better be ready, Aaron's going to throw-up any time now. When he does, it will look like everything inside him has come out."

"What was in the drink, Neen?"

"Some herbs and such to flush out any poison that had made it to the stomach. He'll also have to purge himself from all ends. It will be real messy for about an hour. I'll need all your help to get him to vomit in the bucket and to carry him to the bathroom. I know you're up to it."

The wait is not long. Aaron snaps to a sitting position. Immediately, Neen takes the boy by the shoulders and directs his head to the bucket. Just in time. The flood of fluid and pieces is enormous. Aaron's body bucks and tosses as wave after wave of nausea flushes his stomach. After six or seven waves, Neen again takes Aaron by the shoulders.

"Now to the bathroom. Help me, Michael."

The three walk sideways through the door from the bedroom and the one into the bathroom. Scrambling, the two attendants get the patient to the commode. There follows great rumbling noises, gas explosions and torrents of waste. Aaron is constricted by cramps. He looks like a deflating toy. His facial contortions mirror the distress his body is enduring. The pronouncements from the throne last ten minutes and require four flushes. The odor from the small chamber mixed with the odor from the bedroom begins to gag Michael. Pieces of the paste cast have begun to flake off. The pieces are yellow with pus extracted from the bites in the drying process.

"The most aggressive part is over. Now he needs to rest. I need you to empty the bucket and clean the bathroom so your mother doesn't have to. Bring the bucket back here; there may be some vomiting later. Help me get him back to bed."

The sheets are soaked through to the mattress. Aaron is shivering from a fever and the stress of physical rejection. Twyla Glee sits ready for her part with the ice water filled basin and cloths.

"Keep the cold compresses on him. Put some ice inside the towels to keep them cold. Ruben, put the bible on that chair. I'll need it later. There is nothing any of you can do here. The good nurse and I have everything under control. You can go about your day and check in with us in an hour or so."

Ruben obeys his father. A hint of rejection colors his countenance and his shoulders round. Aaron is his child. He should be the one attending the boy. Silence fills the room as the sun's light fades. Michael and his father finish the unloading, while mother putters in the kitchen waiting anxiously for Dr. Hoffman.

"Twyla, could you spill a little water into the paste and stir it to keep it from drying? I need to apply a new coat to Aaron's wrist."

As Isaac peels away the dried mixture, he notes it is performing its intended duty; drawing the poison from beneath the bites. The caked on mass is almost completely tan underneath, a combination of pus and poison. Maybe one more application is all that will be needed.

"Isaac, I see you are working the farmer's magic. His fever is only 100.5. I can safely assume that it's down in the past two hours. Can I also assume he has vomited, defecated, and urinated substantial quantities?"

"Doctor Hoffman, thank you for coming. I think the worst is over."

The professional and the amateur have respect for each other.

"I'll leave an antibiotic and an antitoxin. You may want to give these to him rather than subject him to another round of bodily rejection. Becky. Rueben. We can talk in the kitchen."

"You saved him, didn't you Grandpa?"

"I only did what I had been directed to do."

At the kitchen table over fresh coffee, the parents want answers.

"I am a country doctor and not a toxicologist. But, I would be willing to guess that the flies carried some form of disease. Or something to which Aaron was susceptible, but Michael was not. Sometimes wasp stings can threaten the life of one child, but not another of the same family. In that case, I recommend the family destroy all the wasps' nests in the area. I recommend that you hunt down and destroy the swarm of black flies. They must nest somewhere near, because they don't have a great flight range. As to Aaron for the present, he appears to be out of danger. Isaac's quick response and basic remedial actions were enough to halt the spread of toxin through Aaron's body. But, and I can't stress this enough, in an ideal world, I would like Aaron in the hospital for close professional observation for the next twenty-four hours. This is not an ideal world, and Isaac is a man of strong beliefs and convictions. He will want to sit with the boy and administer to him through the night. I can abide by that, and so should you. Hopefully, Isaac will give Aaron the medicines every four hours. I urge you to remind him to do so. Other than that, we can wait. Isaac will pray. That will help, too. I must be going. If you need me, call."

It is well past ten when Michael re-enters Aaron's room. Twyla Glee has gone to bed and Mother and Father have paid their last visit to the vigil. Neen sits in the straight-back chair by the bed. The table lamp is all the light in the room. The huge bible is open on his lap and he is praying. His voice is barely audible, but Michael can translate bits and pieces.

Gracious God… lover… innocence… protector… avenger… Lucifer…Great Dragon…sin…death… evil beyond time… love beyond time…loving servant.

Michael is unsure what the fragments mean. These words are parts of phrases Neen chants continuously. He has no idea what the old man is praying. With great force from the heart, the old man is slightly rocking. Michael turns to leave, but is stopped by sudden silence.

"He'll be all right. The poison didn't reach his heart or brain. Go to sleep. We'll talk tomorrow."

The storm is more violent and lasts longer this night. The morning brings Michael's return to his brother's room.

Neen is gone from the chair, but the closed bible is on the bed beneath Aaron's hand. There is color in the patient's cheeks and his breathing is deep and calm. Michael knows the bible must be returned to the glass case. As he delicately extracts and lifts the tome, it slips, and he must clutch the front cover to keep it from falling on Aaron's arm. The leaves and back cover fan open. Startled, he pulls the unwieldy mass to his chest and he sits suddenly in the chair. For the first time in a long time, he stares at the pages after Revelation on which facts and dates are written. The hand that makes the entry changes every thirty or forty years, confirming that this is a living testimony of the family and of the land. Beyond births, marriages, and deaths, political and social events are properly noted.... briefly. The impact of purchases, inventions, governments, and conflicts, from local to international, provide a context for the family commentary. There are no moral judgements, just a notation of facts. There are names, which appear in many generations. Michael is one of the most common. Over the centuries some names were in fashion, and then they seem to have fallen out of favor. Early in the history, the Old World names are prevalent. In the mid-1800's the ancient names disappear.

The handling of the open-paged book causes a piece of parchment to waft to the floor. On the page is written in a precise Gothic script:

> ### *1666 in der Tal Mihai tot bei und mit*
> ### *Genber*
> ### *Chzrut*
> ### *Trelech*
> ### *Nooem*

There are no birth records for these five people, just the year of their death. It's strange that the only mention of them is their first names. Nothing else. No family left behind. Mihai, whoever he was, killed four family members and died at the same time. To kill family is a crime of great evil. What went wrong that this Mihai did this evil thing? It must have been a terrible dispute that got very much out of hand. No wonder the page is torn from the bible. The deed is not something to be proud of. It is strange that the small hex sign after every death date is missing from four of the five. Only Mihai's name is followed by a sign. And it resembles the one on the bottom of the posts. It's the only one like that he has ever seen in the book. Michael finds his own birth record. *Michael Abdiel Hess, born June 6, 1990, Eden Valley, Pennsylvania.*

When he puts the single sheet into the back of the book, he sees there have been other pages before the beginning of the book's history. How many? What is written on the lost leaves? Best return the book to its proper place.

Grandfather is not in the kitchen having coffee. He must be at his house. Michael decides to show Neen the new stones later in the day… after his chores. He and Father are going to string the second electric wire across the fence. The flatbed is loaded with all the right material and tools and hooked up to the little Ford tractor.

"Did you see Aaron this morning?"

"Yes sir. But he was asleep. He looked OK."

"The worst is over. Your mother is relieved. That boy gave us all a big scare."

"Father? You must be proud of Neen for knowing what to do and to do it so fast?"

"Your grandfather is a quite a man. Just like you will be some day. He is a good example to follow. I have tried. Never quite measured up. It bothered me for a time, but I got over it, because I don't think anyone could measure up to him. He never drove me; he just gave me lessons and rules, and the freedom to live my life. I knew he would always be there if I stumbled or did something stupid. But, he never criticized me, even when I was a child. Always asked what I learned from my actions. Hope I have been as good a father to you boys and Twyla Glee as he has been to me."

"I'm honored to be your son."

"And, I'm honored to be your father. You are special. Not like Twyla Glee, you're special in a grown up way. You sometimes act like you were 25 and not 15. The way you speak and think. The knowledge you have and how you've learned beyond high school. The way you care for others. These are the signs of an adult. Your mother and I saw this when you were a small child. Even then you acted a lot like a grown up. Leading and helping. The other children looked up to you and the teachers knew they could trust you. Because you act like an adult, we treat you that way. We even worry a little that you missed parts of your childhood and may be missing your teenage years. That's why we encourage you to go out with your pals and experience this life now. We trust you. We don't worry that you'll get into trouble. We have to keep our eye on Aaron. And, we don't have to take care of you like Twyla Glee. You are more than our child, and your mother and I are honored to be part of your life."

The morning's work goes fast. They are more than halfway completed when they break for lunch.

"Michael, Aaron has been asking after you. Why don't you take your lunch upstairs in his room? Have a nice visit. Be careful not to spill any food."

"Well, big brother, you made it."

"I'd like to know how I got nearly destroyed by the flies and you got nothing."

"Doc Hoffman said it's an allergy. You got it and I don't. It's one of the things that makes us different. Maybe I have an allergy to something that you don't. And if I eat that thing or it touches me, I'll get sick and you won't."

"I guess. One good thing is that I don't have to do any chores for the next few days, until my strength is back. Too bad for you."

"I'll manage. You should have seen the way Neen took control and saved your life. It was like he was the only one who could do it. He was like a general or a doctor in the hospital, bossin' everybody around and runnin' the show. Even Doc Hoffman said he was good. And you know doctors hate to admit someone is better at medicine than they are."

"Thanks for comin' up. I took the medicine about half an hour ago. It makes me really sleepy. I need to take a nap. Come back after your chores, baby brother."

The afternoon is devoted to adding another electric line of warning and protection on the fence. Nothing is more important this day. The wire is attached to a glass condenser on each post about two feet above the first wire. No wolf could climb under or through the two wires. Doubtful a wolf could leap the wire between two open fence slats. That would take a trained animal like in the circus or one of the family dogs.

Aaron and Michael named the dogs, Crash and Bang, based on the way the puppies behaved in the barn. Little balls of fur were always running into walls, hay bales, buckets…whatever was on the floor was fair game for their headlong attacks. At adulthood they were large balls of fur able to break through the old wooden walls of the barn. This was one of their games until Dad placed hay bales around the floor.

Pulik are rare in this part of the world. Originally from Hungary, the breed is the subject of myths, rumors, and just plain lies. Once, Michael saw the dog chart at the vet's office, when he and Aaron took the dogs there for shots. The chart has little pictures of dogs in the land or country from which they originate. Each dog is somehow connected to another, forming links over the entire world. Each dog except the Puli. No one has yet to figure out where these dogs came from or to which other breed they are related. They are that special. They have two coats of hair. The under coat is baby fine and retains body warmth in the winter and snows of the mountains where they herd sheep. To get from one side of a herd to the other, the Puli run over the backs of the moving sheep. There are stories of sheep herders trading six rams and six ewes for one Puli. They are that valuable. A special place by the fire or hearth is always reserved for the Pulik. Adults go without food to ensure the dogs are fed.

The Pulik seem to treat Rebecca and Ruben as animals on a slightly lower rung of the ladder. They would do nothing to harm either adult, but they don't obey them either. Many years ago the big word in the news was *détente*. Father says that is a precise definition of the relationship he and mother have with the dogs.

Crash and Bang are fiercely loyal to the three children. They prefer to be fed by one of them. They have learned not to get under foot while the boys are working, but they follow Twyla Glee wherever she goes. Today they decide to keep Michael company. They lie under the wagon to get out of the sun, and their thick fur becomes matted with dirt, twigs, and grass. As father and son approach the ninth section from the west, the dogs become restless. They pace with their ears laid back. The fur all over their bodies is raised giving them the appearance of bears. They do not growl, but sniff in staccato thrusts as they march like sentries between the posts.

"What's wrong with your friends, Michael? They seem nervous."

"I don't know, father. Maybe there is an animal on the other side of the fence."

"They'd be barking if that was so."

"Maybe they smell the trail left by the animal that killed the Guernsey."

"Yeah that must be it. Just a few more sections to go. Let's not waste time worrying about the dogs."

The last sections are wired in less than two hours. All the while the Pulik stay at section nine, sniff and pace. When the last wire is hooked, it is strung down to the barn on the short metal rods that held the first wire, then hooked up to the transformer. Although the job is complete, the dogs are still at the ninth section. Michael whistles three times the way Neen had taught him. No need to call the dogs' names, they know the whistle. Two large hairy spheres come rushing down the hill. They never once stumble, and are at Michael's feet in a snap. Tongues out, tails wagging hard against the boy's leg, they know it's dinnertime for all the workers.

"I'm going over to see Neen after I help clear the table."

Michael runs up the stairs and gets the newfound stones from their home.

"Aaron, see you in a little while. I'm off to see Grandpa."

It's still light outside. The longest day is not for a few weeks.

"Grandpa. Are you in there?"

"Come on in, Michael."

"You left before I could see you this morning."

"Yes, I wanted to take a brief nap and then get over to see Pastor Zug. We had some things to talk and pray about. How was your day?"

"Father and me…"

"I."

"Yes sir, Father and I set the second wire on the fence posts. It was good to spend time with him. We talked about you. The dogs acted creepy."

"Tell me, did they act strange all the time you were working on the fence?"

"Not all the time. Only at one section. We think it was the section that the wolves came through to kill the Guernsey. The dogs must have smelled the wolves. Maybe they peed on the posts to mark their trail so they could get back to the other side."

"Yes, that must be it."

"I have something to show you, something really special. I found some stones like none I ever saw. Here, take a look and tell me what you think."

Michael lays the black stones on the small table by the easy chair where Neen reads. Nanna gave Neen his own lamp, table, and chair for one of their anniversaries. She knew how much he liked to read the old books. The man's face goes blank, and the color fades from his cheeks.

"Where did you get these stones?"

"I found them."

"Where did you find them?"

The silence is awkward. Michael can hear the breeze blow in the windows and the chair creak on the floor.

"Michael, it's important that you tell me where. I'm not angry and you won't be scolded. I need to know for reasons too complex for you to understand."

"On the other side of the hill. I went to the other side the day after one of the big storms. I found these in a small crater. Then I left the Tal and ran home. Are they special stones, Grandpa?"

"What do you think, son?"

"I think they are. Look! They don't reflect light and they're cool to the touch. You can even squeeze them and they will still be cool. They're special all right. I just don't know how or why."

"They do appear to be special. I can't feel the coolness, but if you say the stones are cool, they must be. My old skin and arthritis affect how I feel things. Leave them here with me tonight. I'll take them over to Pastor Zug in the morning. He is knowledgeable about these things. Together we might figure it out. Now it's getting near your bedtime. You have to do chores for two now that Aaron is laid up. Besides, I'm still tired from sitting up with your brother. I need to get to sleep shortly."

Michael is puzzled and hurt. Neen has been curt. The old man dismisses his grandson like he doesn't matter. Michael knows the old man lives on six hours of sleep. He is a horse. And what did Pastor Zug know about stones anyway?

COOP

The sun's first rays are piercing the black shadows on the land. Crash and Bang are barking furiously and running in circles. Michael follows his father out the door and they see the reason for the commotion.

Fifty or sixty turkey buzzards are circling and diving at the chicken coop farthest from the house. The birds are feasting on stock.

"Good Lord Almighty; what is going on? Michael, get the two 12 gauge shotguns from the cabinet in the barn, and a box of buckshot. Not the birdshot I used on the flies. The big stuff. I'll meet you at the coop."

"Father, it's horrible. Why are the buzzards attacking the chickens?"

"I don't know. They're carrion, they only eat the dead, but they're actually killing… like raptors. And it looks like they started killing before daylight. That never happens. We have to kill them before they do more damage. If we just drive them away for now, they'll be back. Are you ready to shoot like I taught you? Shoot the ones on the ground first. They're the easy targets. You'll get your shooter's eye with them. For the ones in the air, remember to trace a path and shoot in front. About six inches in front for every one hundred feet away. We've got to be quick about it before it gets totally out of hand."

Ruben takes the Winchester six-shot pump and Michael, the Mossberg double barrel. Before they can load and aim, one of the vultures swoops at them. It's so ugly: black and gray feathers, large beak open in the attack, and small head. There is real filth about it. As it comes within ten feet, it is so big, and the attack so sudden that Michael jumps away from the tractor. Crash leaps and snaps at the attacker. The bird swerves, rises, and rejoins the evil flock.

"What, in all that's unholy, was that? "

"Father, why would they attack us?"

"They must be crazed by some thing in nature."

"Do you think they know we are out here to kill them?"

"They're birds, Michael. They don't think, they survive on instinct. Now shoot. And don't worry about the chickens or the coop."

The thunderous blasts echo around the valley. Guts, feathers, and body parts of poultry and buzzard mix on the ground. The men don't have to aim; they just shoot until the target zone is still. The buzzards keep diving. They are eating their own. As they are about to land, the men turn them into exploding blobs, like paper bags filled with wet garbage dropped on the ground. The scavengers turned hunters are so many and so close together, Michael can shoot both barrels at once. He points the gun toward the swirling, flapping mass and fires. Two peel off and dive at the men. Ruben has them in his sights. Pull. Blast. Pump. Pull. Blast. Pieces of the two attackers flop on the ground and in the wire fence. The dogs growl and bark. They move to protect the two gunmen.

"Michael, the ones on the ground aren't going anywhere for a while. We had better start culling the flock in the sky."

The anti-aircraft firing from both guns continues. Those birds not shot from the sky begin to scatter... momentarily, and then regroup. Behind the men, about two hundred feet above their sight, four black angels of death and pestilence are hovering in attack formation. The circle contracts and the swirling accelerates. First one, then the others commence their dive. Crash and Bang know that the threat is real. Their barking and jumping cause Ruben to stop shooting. As he turns to the dogs, he sees the vultures homing in on their prey.

"Michael, stop! Turn and see what's coming our way."

With the reflexes of the hunted, both men train their weapons on the personal threats.

"Look into their eyes and fire, son."

The two muzzles flash. The barrels jerk and one of the birds becomes a thousand pieces. Michael breaks and reloads, while his father keeps up the defense. Pump. Blast. Pump. Blast. Pump. Blast. Two more gone, but one missed. Michael's Mossberg explodes. His shoulder feels the impact. But, the fourth demon is destroyed as pieces of it flutter at the shooters' feet. The foul flock has dispersed and the last ones are seen flying over the top of the hill. There seem to be as many leaving, as there were when the shooting began.

"Ruben. Michael. What's going on here?"

"Dad, that's the damndest thing. The turkey buzzards were attacking the chickens. It must have started before dawn. I've never seen such a thing or even heard of this kind of attack. I mean carrion becoming killers. How's that possible? It goes against their nature."

"Are you both all right? No birds got to you?"

"We're fine, Grandpa."

"Michael was better than fine. He was the best. Must have killed a dozen on the ground and a few in the air. Then he blew two more to smithereens as they were attacking us. And, that's crazy, because birds don't attack hunters. Have you ever heard anything like it, Dad?"

"Never. But, you're safe and unharmed?"

"Yes, we're unharmed. A little sweaty and maybe splattered with buzzard gizzards, but we're safe."

"Ruben, what happened?"

"Becky, it's all right. Let's go back to the house. We can talk about it over breakfast. No sense in staying here now. What's on the ground isn't going anywhere. Michael and I will get to this mess in due time."

"No, son, this mess must be taken care of right away."

"Now, Dad, nothin's going to happen to the body parts and feathers while we have breakfast."

"Ruben, we must clean up the battle remains immediately."

"Father, I say the dead soldiers can wait for a proper burial. And they'll wait."

"If you want to run a risk just to feed your body, I'll take care of it myself. After what you saw with the cow, I think you would want to rid the land of this evil as quickly as possible."

Although he does not raise his voice, the old man pulls himself up to his full height: five feet. The hairs on the back of his neck are on end and his fists are clenched. He has spoken with great intensity. Ruben has heard and is questioning the wisdom of the decision. There is the threat of rebellion. Revolt in front of the woman and children. The air is charged.

34

"Breakfast can wait. Michael, get the wagon, pitchforks, and shovels."

Michael jumps on the tractor and races to the barn.

"Thank you."

"You're welcome."

Each and every bird is forked onto the wagon. The vultures killed over 300 chickens and the men killed more than 30 vultures. The damp topsoil around and under the birds is also dumped on the flatbed. When the clean up is accomplished, Michael and his father take the wagonload of carcasses and debris to the garbage pit for burning. Neen plows the earth with the Deere and covers the turned sod with rock salt. Nothing will live or grow there for years.

"We'll have to move the remaining birds to the other coops, and fence off the battlefield. Do you think that can wait until after we have breakfast, Father?"

"I thought you were never going to have breakfast, son. I mean, you have Michael and me out here working our fingers to the bone for no real good reason, except sanitation. It's been two hours."

The two older men look into each other's eyes and see the warmth of love and accommodation. They walk side-by-side from the barn to the house, like two very close buddies. Michael follows. Maybe someday he would have this kind of bond with his father. Rebecca rushes to the three men.

"Will somebody tell me what that was all about? The shooting and the buzzards. I've never seen so many at one time. Must have been every one in the whole county. It's frightening. I don't like it."

The recounting was brief. Sometimes men don't tell everything. They want to protect their wives and children from what they suspect to be too much or too bad for them to deal with. Isaac and Ruben know what they didn't say could be considered a sin of omission, but they want more time to get answers to their own questions. It's more of a stalling tactic than an intended lie.

The transfer of the remaining poultry to other coops takes most of the morning.

"What do we do with the coop, Father?"

"Let it be for the time being."

"Do you think the buzzards will be back?"

"I don't think so. Your grandfather would be a better person to answer that question. He understands all manner of animal behavior. Here comes Jimmy Hauck."

"Hi, Mr. Hess. Hey Michael, what was all that noise me and my folks heard this morning comin' from your farm? It sounded like World War Three."

"We had some unwanted visitors. Had to shoo them away."

"C'mon, who visits at the crack of dawn? Tell me the truth."

"I've got some paperwork I need to get done and get in the mail. I'll leave you boys to jaw."

Michael's retelling is in much greater detail, with just the appropriate amount of embellishment to make Jimmy jealous.

"You and your dad shot all those buzzards. Holy cow. You're a regular Terminator. That's your new name from now on…Michael 'Terminator' Hess."

"More a protector of those that can't protect themselves."

"And you burned all the vermin and chickens? That's two great gun battles and two great fires over here and I missed both. Dang."

"Mom thinks it must be the phase of the moon that's drivin' the beasts of the land crazy. We're due for a full moon soon, so maybe this is just the start."

"Well I came over to see what happened. I better be leavin'."

"Stay for lunch if you want."

"If it's OK with your mom."

"I'm sure it will suit her fine. She asks about you often. So be ready for a lot of questions."

"I can handle them. "

Jimmy can hardly eat. He's always answering a question. Mom mentions the birthday party and invites Jimmy and his folks. She'll call them. Jimmy leaves right after the meal and before Michael can get any work out of him. The afternoon is filled with makin' sure everything is put back in its place for the next time. Nothin' can drive Father to anger faster than to go for a tool or somethin' he needs and not be able to find it. Aaron is forever not replacing a hammer or pitchfork and father knows whom to ask about it.

"Need any help, Michael?"

"Thanks anyway, Twyla Glee, but there's not much to do and I don't want to run out of work before dinner. Father might find another chore."

"Then I'll go help Mommy ready-up the house and get dinner."

Dinner is pleasant. The prayer offered by father thanks God for his help in ridding the farm of the vultures. Neen's amen is pronounced.

"When you're done helping your mother, Michael, come over to my house for a visit."

Michael does not need a second invitation.

"Neen, what did Pastor Zug have to say about the stones I found?"

"Slow down and I'll tell you everything."

"I took the five pieces to the pastor and he was intrigued by their properties. They're not reflecting light. In fact, the pastor put the stones on his reading table and turned off the light so it was dark in his office. Then he shined a flashlight on the stones, and we noticed that they seemed to absorb the light like little light vacuums. He couldn't feel the coolness you say is there, but he believes you, because you are honest. He got his book geology and tried to look up stones like these. They were nowhere to be found. Stones that absorb light and stay cool in your hand have never been found before by people of science."

"Then he got his book of the ancients; the one that tells about myths, legends, and folklore from all over the world, since man could communicate first symbols, then words. After a long time he read a few pages about people in parts of the Middle East from the time before Jesus. How these people believed that certain stones meant certain things. A stone could be sign or talisman. There were stones for all forms of health and life, for all forms of safety, and victory in battle. Stones were thought to be from the gods, both friendly and unfriendly. Good and evil. These were not just everyday stones, but stones with special properties as they pertain to light, temperature, strength, flexibility, and color. The average person of those regions would walk by the stones and see nothing. Only priests, or shaman as they were called, could interpret the property of a particular stone. Wars were fought over the stones. People died because of a stone's value or because they misinterpreted the property of a stone."

Michael cannot move a finger or blink an eye. He is enthralled.

"One of the very first tribes, who coveted the magic of the stones, believed the stones were fingernails of the earth's spirits. They believed there were spirits living in the trees of the forest and some under the ground. These spirits lived part of their lives under ground and part above ground. In fact, it was the underground spirits that ultimately inhabited the forest and the streams. They had to dig their way to the light from the dark, and in digging, their fingernails were broken. These broken fingernails of the spirits were the stones of power and worth. The book of ancients attempted to tell which stones the tribes revered. Certain colors and compositions, which we today view as beautiful or unique, were, according to the book, viewed the same way by the ancient tribes."

"That's terrific. I found stones, which do not exist, according to modern geology, but they exist as sources of power according to ancient tribes. I knew they were special."

"That's not all. The book mentions *svarz*. Black stones. Completely black. They foretell at least two things. Two opposite things. This is the way it is in interpretations of things old. Even the shaman thought everything had numerous and different meanings. The first possibility mentioned by the book is violence. A black stone is a fingernail of a demon, ordered by the Great Dragon to leave Hades and come to earth. Then the summoned demon moves among the living creatures causing destruction, disease, and famine. The book also offers the interpretation that the black fingernail comes from a powerful demigod and bestows great and eternal power on its finder. Power to rule people and lands, not necessarily in an evil manner, just in a total manner. Like Yahweh's power…absolute and unyielding, the power is."

"You mean I have five fingernails that belong to either the underground gods or the Devil?"

"That is very simplistic. What you have is a mystery according to a book of myths, legends, and folklore. You have stones that are so rare as to be unclassified in a single source of geology. What you have are stones, which should be examined in a sophisticated laboratory."

"My teacher tried that last year, remember. He failed and we sent the stones to State College and all we got was a brush off."

"Pastor Zug knows of a professor at Montana State University in Bozeman, Montana. He says this professor has spent years studying the ancient world and that he has associates in Ankara, Beirut, and Baghdad. If the professor cannot answer questions about these stones, Pastor Zug is confident he knows someone who can. I knew you would want to get to the bottom of this mystery, so I gave the pastor permission to send the stones to the professor.

He sent them to Bozeman by overnight delivery. The pastor will call his friend today. We'll know something soon."

"This is exciting. You and I will get our names in science books. Maybe they'll name the stones after us…like *Blackus Stonus Hessus.*"

Laughter broke the tension of the evening and Michael went home to bed. The storm that night was more severe than the nights before. The lightning seemed to hover over the Tal for thirty minutes. Michael lost count of the strikes at forty-three.

PROFESSOR

"I'm going over to Pastor Zug's this evening, Michael. Ruben, will you let your son accompany me?"

"May I, Father?"

"Just don't be too late. You need your rest. Your grandfather needs a lot less than you do so, don't let him drag you out partyin' 'till all hours."

"Dang, he knows about the party. Michael, can you put your hands on your rock collection and bring it with you."

Neen's truck is not as old as he is, but not by much. Ruben jokes he bought it from Henry Ford personally. But, the old man treats the vehicle like a baby.

"Did Pastor Zug talk to the professor? What did he learn? Why do we need my rock collection?"

"All in due time, Michael. All in due time."

The ride seems to take hours. Michael clutches the bag holding his rock collection. Another larger sack is stowed behind the seat by Neen. They approach the pastor's house, next to the church. Both structures were built by the congregation. The pastor wants for nothing, except riches. The congregation provides food, clothing, transportation, and shelter plus some money each month. They even bought him a computer and hooked him up to the Internet. He is a young man according to Neen, but everyone was young according to Neen. Pastor Zug is really about Ruben's age. The old man and the boy knock and wait.

"It's nice to see you, Isaac, and you, also, Michael. Please come in. I want you to meet my friend, and one of my fondest memories of college, Professor Tomas. He was a student instructor, when I was in college. Helped me over the academic and social rough spots. He always had an eye for the co-eds and they for him. It seems as if there were always two or three hanging on him. I learned a great deal from him. After I graduated, we became reacquainted in Divinity School. It seems we both got the calling at the same time."

Pastor Zug always seems nervous. Tonight he is more than fidgety. He seems to be twitching in anticipation.

"Professor Tomas, this is Isaac Hess and his grandson, Michael."

"How do you do, Sir. Amos has told me much about you. I am honored to make your acquaintance. Michael, I understand you're the reason we're all here tonight. It's a pleasure to meet such an important person."

Handshakes are warm and smiles genuine. Professor Tomas is a black man, a rarity in Michael's world. He tall and solidly built with long arms and legs. He wears baggy shorts with lots of pockets, and a denim shirt with more pockets. His hair is gray and shoulder length in odd-looking long curls. His face is angular and the skin is lined by time outdoors. His eyes behind the wire rimmed glasses are coal black, and his smile shines. Michael is at ease in his presence.

"As I promised, I sent Michael's stones to Professor Tomas for his analysis. He is an anthropologist specializing in the Middle East. Only a few in the world are schooled and trained like Professor Tomas to study people's living habits, cultures, and migrations as they are influenced by the earth's elements and formations. He was so taken by your stones, Michael, that he flew here right away. He asked that we all meet and talk about the stones. Vincent."

"Excuse me, but, you said you know the Professor from college and Divinity School. Is he a pastor or a professor?

"First, please call me Vincent or Vince, whichever makes you comfortable. And that goes for you, too, Michael. I prefer a first name basis. It just makes things easier. Second, I have training as both a priest and a professor. I am no longer active in the church. I am trying to be a scholar. I left the priesthood on good terms. It's just I felt I could do more for mankind as a secular teacher than as a shepherd of a single flock. Now, let me tell you what I know and what I don't know. The stones are very rare because they are not from this part of the world. Their composition is nothing like the elements found in the Mid-Atlantic States. The fact that they don't reflect light is not as rare as many would think. In numerous parts of the world, there are rocks that don't reflect light. And their cool temperature, according to Michael, as opposed to the warm temperature of the environment is also not unique. I have found stones, which maintain temperatures 10- 15 degrees above their ambient surroundings and some, which maintain temperatures, 10-15 degrees below their surroundings. All of that said, the combination of the attributes is unique to this part of the world. The issue of reflection, as well as the indicated temperature of the stones, tells me you have found something very special. I must say indicated temperature, because I am unable to detect the coolness that Michael claims. But, Amos vouches for both of you, so I am inclined to believe the temperature issue for the moment."

"By special, do you mean that in a geological way or some other way? And, please call me Isaac. What do you make of the fact that only Michael can feel the coolness?"

"Isaac, as of now, we have a geological phenomenon. Nothing more. As to Michael's ability to sense the different temperature, I have no scientific way to confirm or refute that is real or imagined, so I'll take Michael's sensation on faith. Faith still plays a big part in my life."

Neen does not seem disappointed.

"Michael, did you bring your other stones for Vincent?"

"Yes, Pastor, they're here in this bag."

"If you don't mind, I'd like to examine them tomorrow morning. It will take a great deal of concentration and I've had a long day. My body is going through the wobbles of time-zone change. Isaac, did you bring the family bible?"

"Here."

"I don't want you and Michael to be disappointed. A discovery such as this could be important. I just need time to review all the information, before I feel confident enough to go to any national or international scientific associations for excruciating tests and confirmation of my hypotheses."

"Vincent, did Pastor Zug tell you about the cow being slaughtered and the flies? And the buzzards' pre-dawn attack on the chickens. And did he tell you about the ferocious thunder and lightning storms that come every year? Except this year they are much worse. About how the storms seem to rain lightning into the Tal?"

Isaac is pleading for the evening to continue.

"Isaac, please tell me what you know and what you suspect. Amos may have left out some detail. I need all the facts I can get before we go to the next step. I'll take notes."

Neen recounts everything, even the smallest fact. Plus, a lot of his feelings, things Michael had not heard.

"That's about it. Do you have any questions?"

"Not right now, and thank you, Isaac."

"It's getting late and I must get Michael home. He needs his beauty sleep. You know children. Are you staying here at Pastor Zug's house?"

"Yes, I know children. No, I'm staying at the Dutchland Motel. I need space for my work and I work strange hours, because of my international associates and my staff at the university are all in different time zones. I didn't want to disturb the Pastor and his normal workload."

Neen and Michael are pensive on the way home. The old man is slightly pessimistic and the boy is confused.

"Watch out, Grandfather!"

With that warning, the truck swerves to avoid hitting something that is standing in the middle of road. The truck bounces into the ditch and comes to a precarious stop before a large elm.

"What in the name of all that's holy was that?"

"A cow?"

"No cow."

"A deer? A big buck?"

"No deer in this part of the state in thirty years."

"Bales of hay?"

"What fool would leave hay in the middle of the road without a light to warn others? Whatever it was, it wasn't here when we went to Amos Zug's."

"It wasn't a man. Nobody is that big. It was about three times bigger than that professor."

Michael's pulse has shot up to the real fear level. Neen is breathing too heavy. He doesn't sound good.

"Are you OK to drive home, Grandpa? I could do that for you if you're too disturbed."

"I'll be fine in a few seconds. Get out and guide me out of this mess. Tell me if I should back out, or just go straight onto the road."

"It looks like you have a clear path to the road by going forward after you turn around the tree. I'll walk in front lookin' for rocks and holes."

Gingerly the old man guides the truck up the embankment onto the road.

"I want to go back and see if we can see any trace of what was on the road."

"There's the spot. I remember as we were comin' over the little rise there were six trees in a row beside the road where the thing was standin' or sittin'."

"Grab the flashlight from under your seat, son. We need to examine the area."

"I think it was right about here, Neen."

"There's nothing there now. Not a trace of anything ever having been there. Let's check the roadsides. See if it left a trail. We'll walk about twenty feet in front and twenty feet behind where we saw it."

"Nothin' on either side. No grass pushed down or stones turned over, except where we went off the road. So nothing could have run away."

"Check the embankment. Maybe it jumped from the road."

"Nothin'. No marks on the ground."

"Could it have been some of your school chums pulling pranks late at night? This road gets busy some times."

"I doubt it Grandfather. They're too chicken to risk their lives for a joke. But, feel this."

"What did you find?"

"Nothin' but cold air. Feel how cool it is in this spot of the road. Outside of this area, the air temperature is warm like you'd expect for a June night, but here the air is cooler. Can you feel it?"

"No. I can't feel any difference in the air from one place to another on the road. We had better get home. Your father will be mad at me if I keep you out too late."

Why would Neen lie? The air in the spot was a lot cooler than the rest of the air.

The storm starts early tonight. The lightning bolts are striking the earth inside the Tal again.

The knock on the door stirs Michael awake. The whisper is out of place.

"Michael, wake up, it's me, your grandfather. We need to get going."

"Going where Neen?"

"Get dressed and I'll tell you. But, be very quiet."

Groping and grabbing for jeans, shirt, socks and work boots, Michael is through his bedroom door and down the stairs in less that three minutes. In the kitchen he is handed a mug of coffee. Grandpa style: black and strong enough to peel paint off the barn. The first sip burns the boy's lips. He blows before taking the second.

"Why are we in such a hurry and why so sneaky?"

"I'll leave a note that we went fishing before the sun came up. You have to promise you'll back up the note to your folks."

"I promise. Where are we really going?"

"The pastor and the professor are over at my place. They want all of us to go into the Tal. Now."

"It's still pitch dark. What time is it?"

"Three. Now let's get going."

"How will we get into the Tal without setting off the alarm and breakin' the fence?"

"I turned off the alarm. We will reset it when we return. We can pry loose one of the planks and slide through. You can do that can't you, Michael?"

"Yessir."

"One more big gulp of coffee, then we're out the back door."

"Good morning, Michael."

"Morning Pastor. Morning Vincent."

"We brought flashlights for you two. Michael, you lead because you know the fastest path to the fence."

The expeditionary force arrives at section nine and Michael pries loose the same planks he pried and re-nailed. The four slide through the gap. Vincent struggles because of his girth and large backpack.

"Now where do we go?"

"To the right of the stand of trees is a narrow path that leads down to the base of the Tal. It can be slippery and overgrown, so be careful."

Negotiating the way down the other side is difficult. Twice the pastor falls and has to be helped up. Once Vincent's backpack gets snagged in some massive bushes and the thorns cut him. With Vincent, Michael walks ahead of the other two.

"Where exactly did you find the stones?"

"Over there in the open field, just to the right of the building."

"Did you look anywhere else?"

"No, sir, I just grabbed them and ran. I was scared. Did I do wrong?"

"No, Michael, you did not do any wrong."

"Amos, you and Isaac look around. Take nothing except notes. Michael and I will go to the building. Best not linger, but be as thorough as you can. Quickly now."

"Vincent, what is this building? It's too small for a barn. Is it a house like where my grandfather lives?"

"Sort of. My guess is that it is or was a monastery. A religious meeting hall of sorts. See the stone walls. They have no windows. And the walls and roof seem to be locked together like they are one piece, as if to make the structure impenetrable. I'll wager there is only one entrance and it is in the shape of an arch. The building is in the middle of the space. Why not placed against one of the earthen walls of the Tal? There has to be a reason for its placement."

Michael moves closer to Vincent.

"Don't be afraid. We're safe. Look above the arch."

Berg Alle Gotten

"I know from the bible that berg means mountain."

"Yes, Michael, and it also means fortress or Keep. The words mean 'A fortress of the gods'. The building was a Keep. A Keep is the safest place to hide within a castle. When the castle was being stormed, the Keep was that place where the men hid the women, children, and valuables from the invading forces."

"Why a fortress or a Keep?"

"That's what we need to learn. Let's go into the building. Tell me what you see and feel. Be careful you don't trip or fall. And don't disturb anything."

"Nothing but an altar. I can see its outline by the moonlight from the door. The wall by the doorway was at least three feet thick. This was a Keep for sure. Feel how cool it is in here. The floor seems to be solid. I can't determine if it is all one slab or just tightly packed boulders. That's about it. This is a chapel, as well as a Keep."

"A room for religious rites. Do you see that the altar is on a platform about eight feet above the base floor?"

"Yessir. But, havin' the altar higher is common in churches. At least the ones I've been in."

"Not eight feet higher."

"Do you think there is anything under the altar floor? Should we check or will that disturb something? You should see this altar. It's not like anything I've ever seen. It's made of a solid piece of stone. And the stone is dark like the stones I found, but it reflects the beam from my flashlight. What looks like a shallow basin is carved into the top. And there is a funnel like opening from the basin. If I follow the downward path from the funnel, the stream enters a hole between two wide dark planks. Beyond the altar, there is something in the wall. It looks like a metal plate about two feet across and three feet deep. There is some very strange writing on the plate. I've never seen this kind of writing."

"Michael, don't touch the plate, until I get to you."

"Neen, I'm all right. I'm just lookin'."

"Professor, I think I've seen some of these words before. I can't make out the details, because of the bad light and the dirt on the plate. But, I think I recognize four names: *Genber, Chzrut, Trelech,* and *Nooem.* They are inscribed within what looks like a star. It is located at the top and center of the plate. And there appears to be a fifth name...*Mihai.* This last name is inscribed upside down outside the star at the bottom of the plate.

"Don't touch the plate, either of you. Wait for me. Just stay there. Amos. Come to us. Hurry."

Vincent climbs up the ladder to the altar floor and stands directly in front of the plate.

"I need to take a photo of the inscription so I can decipher it on my computer."

He takes digital photos from five different angles and two distances. Then he takes a knife and scrapes off a sliver of the plate and puts it into a glass vial, which he drops in his backpack.

"This is terrific. We don't have much time to explore the area around and beneath the altar. Let's go. The gap between the two planks is wide enough for our fingers. Michael, if you lift from that side, I'll lift from this. We ought to be able to pry the board away or move it enough that we can see underneath."

"On the count of three. Ready. One. Two. Three. Aghhh. Again. One. Two. Three. Ugghh. One more and we'll have it. One. Two. Three. Ugghh. Got it."

The shafts of moonlight reflect the sweat and straining muscles. The large plank has been pulled up and banged off to the side. The second one goes easier. Then it hits all four men. The stench coming from beneath the altar is a combination of rotten flesh and animal waste. And it is like steam. Air from the underground should be cool. The building is cool.

"Oh my God. What is that foul odor?"

"Neen, it smells like the Guernsey before we set fire on it. There must be some dead animals down there. Maybe they crawled under the floor, during one of the storms and couldn't get out. Then they starved to death. I want to see."

"Michael there may be something down there not meant to be seen."

"But, we're here to examine."

"Vincent, I'll go with my grandson. You sure couldn't fit through the opening and Amos, you're just not brave enough."

"It's deep, Grandfather. I just dropped a penny and I never heard it hit anything."

From his backpack, Vincent pulls two lengths of climber's rope.

"Tie these around your bodies. Amos and I will lower you through the opening and stand ready to pull you up instantly. I doubt if you'll go to the bottom, but you'll be able to look around."

As they are tying their halters under their legs and around their hips, Vincent removes a small vial from his shirt pocket. He goes first to Michael and then to Isaac. Opening the vial, he puts his thumb over the mouth and upends it. Liquid remains on his thumb. He touches each of them on the forehead, making the sign of the cross. Then he puts the vial away. Slowly the Hesses are lowered under the altar. Amos and Vincent wrap each rope around the altar to control the process.

"That's about ten feet. Can you see anything?"

"Nothing but the sides of earth. It's round like a giant well or tunnel. I can't tell if it's man made or natural. The heat and smell seem are more intense."

"We'll let the rope out some more. You can't go deeper than thirty feet. Talk to us as you descend."

"Wait. Ah, dang. I thought I saw a rat. But, it couldn't be a rat. It was too big. It looked to be the size of a wild cat. Maybe thirty pounds. There don't seem to be any holes for it to hide in. Must have been a shadow that tricked my imagination."

"Vincent, I see something on my side."

"What do you see, Michael?"

"It looks like the end of a coffin or maybe a small door. Swing me over to the right, I want to check."

"No!"

Vincent's raspy bass voice catches everyone by surprise.

"Why not?"

"Don't touch anything down there. Stay in the center and observe. When we come back we can explore further. This time is just to see where we are going. It's time to come up. Can you pull Isaac, Amos?"

"He's quite heavy, I can barely hold him."

"Steady him until I get Michael up."

"Isaac, we're going to bring up Michael first. Can you hold on for a few more minutes?"

"I'll just hang around. Sorry, I couldn't resist the levity."

While Vincent is extracting Michael, Isaac has the opportunity to explore the side of the tunnel nearest him. The three of them hoist the old man.

"Let's get out of here. I need to get back to the motel and log onto my computer. We must put back the planks."

As the others are leaving, Vincent tilts water from the vial and makes the sign of the cross on the planks and the altar.

"Vincent, look at the field. Even in the dark, I can see a lot of craters. These are like the ones in which I found the stones. Let's check for more stones."

"All right. We'll spread out and look for stones. Amos, you and Isaac look around, too."

Vincent sees the crab apple tree for the first time. For *genus malus cultivars*, it is huge, at least fifty feet high. It is barren of fruit, and has few leaves, but the twisted trunk and limbs unmistakably confirm its family. Strange that the branches, although gnarled and convoluted, all seem to reach upward. This is rare for crab apple. Vincent cuts away a small piece of bark and stuffs it in his pack.

"Over here, Vincent. Look. Three more stones. They're not black. They are a dark red-brown like they are filled with iron ore. Let's take these. You can examine them later. No stones anywhere else around the chapel. Just these three."

"Only burnt shreds of bark and bunches of grass in these craters."

"Grab some of each and bring it along."

The four scramble back up the hill and through the gapped planks. Neen re-nails them in their proper place.

"Michael, you'd best go home before the sun rises and your folks see you're missing. I'll go to the barn and turn on the electric fence. We'll go over to Pastor Zug's this evening. We need to understand what we saw. Just not now."

CISTERN

A single drop of water hangs delicately from every spigot and tap in the house. Around the drains of sinks, showers, and tubs, befouled fluid has been collecting almost imperceptibly for a few hours. The small pools are comprised of yellow and brown swirls. In the bathrooms and above the kitchen sink, the air is heavy with a stench; a combination of sulfur and burnt protein. The stink has begun to permeate the house. Ruben is the first to stir. A biological clock awakens him before sunrise. It's as if he is the one to get the day started. He plods to the bathroom. Frozen at the door, he gags. Gasping a breath of hallway air, Ruben quickly steps into the bathroom and finds the source of the airborne discomfort.

"Becky, get up."

"Is the coffee ready?"

"I haven't been down stairs yet. Get up. We need to talk."

"What's the problem?"

"There's a terrible smell in the bathroom."

"What?"

"There is a terrible smell in the bathroom, and it seems to be coming from the water."

Becky blinks and stares at her husband.

"What can we do?"

"First of all, no one is to use or draw water until we have a clear understanding of the problem. Please awaken the children and tell them."

"I can smell something already. Is that coming from the bathroom?"

"Yes, it's spreading rapidly."

"Did you check the boys' bathroom? Maybe it's just ours."

Ruben is dressing quickly. Becky follows suit. The rank odor has taken over the second floor of the house.

"Aaron? Michael? You have to get up now. Your father needs your help."

"Pfeeu, what died?"

"Just get up and find your father."

"Michael, did an old weasel crawl inside you last night and die? Is it your gas that smells so bad?"

"Aaron, please do as I ask. Boys, your father thinks there is something wrong with the water, so don't wash, get a drink, or use the toilet until he knows for sure."

The boys scramble to dress and put on their shoes.

"Twyla Glee, get up honey. I need your help right away."

"Mommy, what's that terrible smell?"

"Your father and I don't know. He and your brothers are going to find out, while you and I try to get breakfast ready without water."

"No water?"

"Your father thinks the smell is coming from the water, and he asked that we not use any water until he is sure it is safe."

"Safe?"

"Just a precaution, honey. We wouldn't want anybody to get sick, now would we?"

The entire household is in motion. Ruben and the boys go from room to room to confirm the extent and intensity of the intrusion. The two women are setting breakfast on the picnic table. There is no coffee.

"Dad, we found the stink in the basement sink, so I guess it's all over the house."

"But, the smell is not coming from the drains."

"How can we be sure?"

"Father, I leaned over and sniffed the spigot. The smell was real strong. Then I sniffed the drain, and the smell was not as strong. The smell was at the drain, but it was from the water that had collected there."

"We better confirm this everywhere in the house. If what you say is true, we don't have a septic tank back up, we have a very serious water supply problem. Back to the house, boys. This time cover your mouths and noses until you are in a bathroom, just to be very safe."

"Thanks a lot, baby brother."

Handkerchiefs in hand and in place, the three men re-enter the house. By now, the foul air has conquered the living space. Six eyes are red and tearing within three minutes. The men sit hard on the picnic benches coughing in the exchange of indoor air for outdoor air.

"Michael, run over to your grandfather's house and warn him. Tell him our water supply is fouled and he must not use any water until we solve the problem. Aaron, go to the barn and check the water coming in there. I'm going to the stream. We can eat when we get back."

Michael is half way to Neen's before Ruben is finished. Aaron sulks and trudges off.

"Mommy, I'm scared. What's the matter?"

"Twyla Glee, everything will be just fine. Your father has everything under control."

Becky's darting eyes and fidgeting with her apron belie her calm words. She has no idea what's going on, and this disruption is disconcerting.

"No smell from the barn, dad. The cows will be safe. We can drink that water, can't we?"

"The creek seems to be untouched. I think we can drink the water in an emergency."

"Ruben, this seems like an emergency."

"Not yet."

In silence, all five inhale breakfast. Isaac strides purposefully to the table.

"My house has a terrible odor. What's wrong?"

"Isaac, I don't know, but I want to find out before the situation gets much worse. We know the smell comes from the water, so it's a supply problem and not a waste problem."

"Ruben, it could be that the septic tank broke and the seepage is spoiling the water that comes from the well. It could be that seepage is fouling the well or just the pipe from the well."

"I doubt that any seepage could be fouling the well. The top of the well is eighty feet deep. The bottom of the septic tank is twenty feet deep. Also, the septic tank is a hundred yards from the house and the well is directly beneath it. So, the earth and rocks would filter any seepage as it drained down toward the well. The seeping fluid would be cleansed by the time it got to the water source for the well."

"We have to make one more visit to the houses, barn and creek. We must get samples of water from each tap. We'll use jars from the pantry. After you get a sample, put the lid on the jar and twist it real tight. Make sure the seal is hard. Then we'll take the samples to the County Water Department. I'm sure they can run some kind of test on the water and tell us what has happened. Let's go. The faster we get this done, the sooner we can go back to normal."

The jars are wrapped in an old sheet and carefully placed in a cardboard box. As Ruben steps into the truck's cab, he discusses the day's chores with his sons, and the importance of staying away from the fouled water. The drive to the county services building takes twenty minutes. The muted clinking of the bottles reminds Ruben how pock marked and bumpy are the county roads. More than once, he glances into the box to be sure nothing has broken.

"Good morning, may I help you?"

"Yes, please. I think my well is contaminated and I need someone to help me understand the problem and explain how to get rid of the contamination."

"The last door on the left down at the end that hall. That's the Water Department. I'm sure someone can help you there."

Ruben's paces echo in the empty tile-covered hall. He holds the carton in front of him like a precious gift. Negotiating the door entrance without risking dropping the box is not possible. He knocks.

"Yessir. How can we help you?"

"My well is contaminated. I brought samples of the water from all the taps for you to examine. I don't know the type or cause of the contamination, and I need someone to explain how to get rid of it."

"Let me have the box. Come with me."

Ruben delicately hands over his parcel. The two men walk into a small laboratory.

"My name is Bill Snyder. And you are…?"

"Ruben Hess. I live over in Eden Valley. Isaac Hess is my father."

"Yessir, I know the farm. It's on the other side of the hill from the Tal. Here, sit beside me, while I examine what you brought."

"Be careful opening the jars. The water is very foul smelling."

"Yessir."

The technician opens each jar and removes a few drops, which he places on a glass slide, covers with another piece of glass, and notes the source. Each slide is placed on the platform of a microscope and viewed by the technician.

"I'm examining each sample to see if there are any irregularities in the water. This is a basic and very quick analysis, but with it we can spot 90-95% of any foreign bodies in the medium. If a more detailed examination is needed, I'll send the samples to Harrisburg. They have a system that is ten times more powerful than ours here. However, the complete analytical process takes two days."

"We can't wait two days. This is our water supply. And the stench makes living in the house impossible. We need to get to the problem and eliminate it now."

There is no patience in Ruben's voice or demeanor. He waits for what seems like thirty minutes while Bill Snyder examines each sample and makes corresponding notes.

"Whew, you were right. The water stinks. And here is the reason. Take a look. See those worm-like entities swimming in the water. There are maggots in the drinking water, but not in the creek or the water from the barn. The maggots are also in the water in your father's house."

"Maggots. How is that possible?"

"Since dead carcasses are the optimum media for maggots, something must have gotten into your well and died."

"The well is very deep below the house, and the entrance to it in the basement is appropriately capped. Nothing could have gotten into the well from the basement."

"Could some animal gotten into the well from the shaft beneath the house?"

"The shaft is stone and mortar for twenty feet. I don't know of any animal that lives in hard earth twenty feet below the surface."

"Moles and a few other tunneling rodents have been known to go pretty deep."

"Not likely twenty feet."

"Mr. Hess, I can only tell you what I've found here in the lab. If you'd like I can accompany you home and we can examine the well cap and shaft."

"I'd appreciate that."

"One last item, sir. Did you contact any of your neighbors to see if they have a similar problem?"

"Not yet."

"I suspect that if they have the same problem, they would be here by now or on their way. If they don't have the problem, there is no need to alert them to nothing. It could only cause them to become concerned. Let's look at your well before we do anything else. I need to load a truck with supplies and equipment. It will only take a few minutes. I'll follow you to your farm."

"Thank you, Mr. Snyder. I'd like to get to my family. I'm sure they're worried."

Ruben's return to the farm is less pressure-filled than his trip to the Water Department. An understanding of the issue and help at solving the problem ease his mind. The white van with the state seal on the door arrives ten minutes after Ruben.

"Mr. Snyder, this is my father, Isaac, my two boys, Aaron and Michael, my wife, Rebecca and our daughter, Twyla Glee. Folks, this is Bill Snyder, from the county Water Department. He's come to help us discover the source of the problem."

"We need to get to the well cap."

"It's in the basement. You had better cover your mouth and nose. The smell is terrible in the house."

"Thanks. Mr. Hess, I'll need you to go with me."

"Can we go, too?"

"If you want to."

"Ruben, I'll stay here with Becky and Twyla Glee. No need for a gang of investigators."

"Thanks, Neen."

The four men with bandana masks enter the kitchen door and descend the stairs to the basement. Lights are turned on as the posse moves from space to space. The concrete floor is damp and there are spider webs in every corner. This part of the basement is infrequently visited. The door to the water room is ajar and easily opened. The putrid odor makes all four men gasp.

"The source of the problem is close. Where is the well cap?"

"Next to the water tank. We draw water from the well; it goes into the tank and is softened. The pallets holding the bags of water softener pellets will have to be moved for you to get to the cap. Boys?"

Bags are shifted onto one pallet, and it is removed to reveal two metal plates, which seem to cover a four-foot square space. There is a three-inch pipe centered where the plates meet. This pipe feeds the large tank. Aaron and Michael lift the plates and Bill Snyder kneels over the opening. He lowers a small jar attached to a long filament. Finally he withdraws the jar filled with water. He caps the jar and places it, next to one of the jars Ruben had brought to the lab, on a white piece of paper. He shines a very intense light on both jars.

"That's strange."

"What?"

"The water color and apparent composition in the two containers is different."

"What do you mean different?"

"Mr. Hess, look closely. The jar you brought to the lab has a dark yellow hue …almost tan. The water I just extracted from the well has no such discoloration. It's clear. We know that the maggots cause the yellow color in the water you retrieved. So, no yellow color should mean no maggots in the well. That's what is strange. There are maggots in the water, but apparently none in the water source."

"Father, look. The lid to the tank is not closed."

Ruben stands and quickly moves to the tank. The lid, through which the pellets are introduced is, indeed, partially open.

"Sir, let me get a sample of water from the tank."

Lifting the lid allows a near cloud of stench to fill the room. Bill Snyder begins to pale. Michael notices a few lethargic large black flies escape from the opening. Michael and Aaron swat and kill the slow moving intruders. The color of the water sample from the tank matches the color of the water Ruben had jarred.

"There's the problem, sir. Something, carrying the maggot larvae, got into the water tank and died. The maggots came to life and infested your water supply. Now that we know the source of the problem, it can be solved. I suggest you seal off the pipe to the well to the tank, as well as the exit pipe from the tank. Then you can clean the tank. Until the tank is cleaned, sterilized, and reconnected, you'll have to get drinking and bathing water from elsewhere. I'm going to take these two samples back to the lab. I'll call you after I've analyzed the water. Now, if you don't mind, I must leave before I wretch."

With his family at the table, Ruben explains what was discovered. He and Isaac will go the Hunsecker Mill Store and buy a twenty-five gallon water tank for immediate hook up. They will order a larger tank to replace the one now in the basement. The boys will empty the large tank and pour the water on the driveway stones to evaporate. The maggots will die in the sun. Once the large tank is empty, it can be dismantled and discarded.

"Before we leave, I want to know who was the last one to put pellets in the tank."

"I was. But, I remember putting the lid back on the top and screwing it down tight. I remember this because I turned it so the scratch mark on the lid matched up to the scratch on the tank. Just like you showed me when I first did the chore. Father, I'm sure of it."

"Michael, the lid could not have unscrewed itself, and I doubt if Aaron went down to the basement and unscrewed the lid. I know that didn't do it. So, the only explanation is that you forgot to properly perform your task. And, your family nearly suffered for your carelessness. Correcting for your error will be costly and time consuming."

"Father, believe me, I screwed down the cap. I swear."

"Son, I'm disappointed, but not angry. Now, we need to get to work."

STONES

Michael rounds the barn and sees them hanging by their necks with their bellies ripped open. Crash and Bang have been butchered. The boy freezes, and then explodes.

"Dad. Aaron. Come quick. Something's happened to the dogs."

The double slam of the screen door heralds the arrival of father and son.

"What in God's name happened here?"

"Somebody killed the dogs."

"Michael, I can see that. I want to know how. And why? It had to be somebody they knew; else they would have put up a terrible fight. We would have heard the noise. Look at the carcasses, they've been gutted. Nothin' inside except ribs and flesh. Their privates are mutilated. Not cut off. The tops of their heads have been peeled back. Looks like their brains were removed, but there's no blood on the ground around the bodies."

"And no foot prints. There would have to be foot prints when the person that killed them hung them up on the tree limb."

"You boys cut them down. Then Michael, you take them to the pit for burning. We can't let Twyla Glee see this. It would disturb her something fierce. Aaron, come back to the breakfast table. After breakfast we've got to figure out what in God's name is going on."

Breakfast was silent, despite pointed questions from Mom. The three men met in the barn.

"Boys, all of this death and destruction is very troubling. With the cow, it could have been a pack of wolves from the other side. Then the buzzards attacked the chickens. Buzzards don't attack living creatures, and they don't feed before dawn. Now the dogs: gutted and mutilated with no sign of their body parts or the people who killed them. I'm not frightened. I am very upset. Somehow, someway, we have to get to the bottom of all this. And we have to do it now. Aaron, you've been in bed these past few days, so I don't expect you to have many ideas. Michael, what do you think about all this?"

Ruben is no longer speaking calmly or quietly, he was almost yelling.

"Well, Neen and I…"

"I knew the old man was involved in this somehow. But, he wouldn't destroy livestock. What does he have to do with all this?"

"I found some stones, and he gave them to Pastor Zug, who sent them to Professor Tomas in Montana, who flew here and I met him at the Pastor's house."

"What do stones have to do with this? Son, you are not making sense."

"They're from the ancient time and they mean either evil or good they're very powerful magic I found them over the hill this morning the four of us went back we found a well and some more stones they were dark red-brown and they weren't cold like the black ones Professor Tomas… Vincent took the stones so he could examine them and work on his computer."

"Michael, slow down and take a breath. I'm not angry with you. I just want to get to the bottom of these mysteries and stop further carnage. I think we should talk to your grandfather and see what he has to say."

"You're in deep trouble, baby brother."

"Shut up, Aaron. You don't have the foggiest idea what this is all about."

"Isaac? Are you in there? We need to talk. The boys and I are worried about the slaughter of the livestock. Could you come out here?"

"No need to yell. I can hear you just fine. Now what is it that you want to jaw about? I'm kinda busy getting' Michael's birthday gift ready, so give me a few minutes. Now what seems to be the problem?"

"Dad, you know very well what the problem is. First the Guernsey, then the chickens, and this morning we found the two dogs gutted and hanging from a tree. It's like we are under attack. Michael tells me he found some stones of some kind, and they were sent to some professor, who is at Pastor Zug's. He also said that you took him over the hill this morning before breakfast, but you left a note that you were going fishing. You are not a liar. So you're trying to keep something from Becky and me. What is going on? What is all the mystery? Why are the animals being butchered? I need answers."

"I don't have answers. I have very few facts and a great many thoughts and feelings. I have maybes and what ifs. That's why Amos sent for the professor. To get answers for something we didn't understand. I can tell you this: whatever is happening is most likely not what it seems and for sure is more important than the death of the livestock. I think we had better go to the pastor's house to learn more."

As they were leaving, Michael noticed dirt on the floor of Neen's house near the rocking chair. This house was always spotless. Ruben had commented more than once that he thought the house was a little too clean. Michael asked himself why dirt there and not from the front door in? Then the boy saw two black twisted roots on the table by the rocker.

The pastor and Vincent were sitting at the dining table, examining the stones from Michael's collection. Holding them, rubbing them one against another, shining a bright small light on them, and peering at them through a special magnifying lens. Ruben's knock on the door startled the two scholars.

"Pastor, I don't intend to butt in, but given the recent butcheries and my son's actions this morning, I demand to know just what is going on and where will all this lead?"

"Please come in. You're right, we all need to talk. Let me introduce Vincent Tomas, Doctor of Anthropology at Montana State University. Vincent this is Ruben Hess and his elder son, Aaron."

Gracious and warm... ever the man of God.

"Good day to you, Mr. Hess and Aaron. Please call me Vincent. It makes things go more easily. Please sit around the dining table. It's conducive to conversation."

"Would anyone like herb tea?"

Six cups.

"Professor... Vincent, allow me to start."

In as much detail and as little embellishment, Ruben relates all that he knows has occurred in the past few days. Vincent takes notes. The mugs are half-empty.

"That is very interesting and it fills in several blank places on my canvas. There are still many questions to be raised, but I am getting an idea as to the magnitude and import of this time. Do you all see these stones? Let me tell you what they tell me."

Vincent details the meaning of the black stones for the benefit of Ruben and Aaron. His notes are copious. Then he isolates the stones Michael found during last year's forays into the Tal.

"The blue one with the red strata, the purple and pink one, the light green and brown one, and the jagged yellow and white one are unique. Their composition is not of this area. Not even of this country. There could be any one of a dozen reasons to support a dozen hypotheses about the composition and meaning of these stones. Suffice it to say they represent four different yet related factors, forces, or entities. Different because they are different. Different in color and striation. Related in location of discovery, hardness, and reflective quality, yet vastly different from the black stones, which share the location yet a different reaction to light. The black stones reflect no light, but these four do. But, the reflection is not a true angular light response, as one would anticipate. The light appears to strike the four multi-colored stones and to be refracted or bent in a haphazard manner. It matters not at what angle or what place the light strikes. It is bounced away as if it were a threatening element. I suspect if we had a complete laboratory, we could determine if the light were being deflected at the same speed that it strikes. And no two deflections are the same. Almost as if the stones were deflecting it away in any direction they wished. Imagine an ancient warrior shielding himself against arrows. The arrows come at any time, from any direction and with all manner of intensity. The warrior holds his shield to protect his head and heart and moves it in anticipation of the arrows' onslaught. The arrows are bent or broken upon striking the shield and they ricochet away in a haphazard manner. Or they simply glance the shield and slide off harmlessly. The stones seem to have the protection of some sort of shield."

"Excuse me, sir, I don't know you well enough to josh with you, nor am I nearly as learned as you are. But, since we are talking about things that affect my son and father, I must tell you my reaction is balderdash. How in the name of God and nature could a stone think or react? Stones are inanimate objects. No life, no feelings, no senses, no soul. You are giving these properties to four pieces of compressed earth. It simply can not be. There has to be a logical reason for the reaction of the light to the stones and not the illogical one you give for the stones' response to the light."

"Sir, I understand your skepticism. It is normal and natural. Believe me when I say that were I in your position, I would react in the same manner. But, there are many things above and beyond our experiences and reasoning. I cannot fully explain what we are noticing with the stones and light. At least I cannot explain it in terms, which we would all understand. Let me ask you, do you believe in God?"

"Yes I do. I'm a God fearing man."

"Sir, I am not being flippant, but do you believe in a supreme or superior anthropomorphic good or do you have unverifiable faith in a power beyond human power to which you ascribe the term, God? Does your God have human-like attributes and properties, or when you reference God do you reference only power?"

"I am not schooled to get embroiled in a religious argument with you, Sir. I believe in God."

"Your faith is unshakable. Hold tight to that. Hold on for dear life."

"I will."

"This morning, we enjoined an early morning expedition to the Tal."

Vincent details the activities of the four explorers. Referring to his notes, nothing is left out. He comes to the three dark red-brown stones Michael found in a crater. The subjects of this part of the retelling are pushed away from the others on the table.

"These are different from the multi-colored stones and vaguely similar to the black ones in that they are singular in color, composition, and density. Plus, they absorb light like the black ones, and, according to Michael, they are cool to the touch. As you know, neither Amos nor I can feel the coolness. Here is the truly intriguing characteristic of these three. They are changing color. By that I don't mean that they are changing color in reaction to light or its absence, changes in temperature, pressure placed on them, or proximity to the other stones. I mean their color is changing. When we got them to the house, I scanned them into the computer, separately, as I had done with the others. About an hour ago, I thought I noticed a change in color, or rather color density. They seemed to have gotten darker. So I rescanned them and on the screen, I compared the two scans. The three had become darker during their stay in the house. Although it may be that they are inside and not outside. Or the light from the scanner may have altered the color of the stones. I doubt that is possible, because the light is absorbed. That being the case, the scanner light would have brightened or lightened the stones. No. It is the opposite. Light is making them darker. It's as if they were changing. Evolving. Becoming something of a different color. Yet not changing their composition, their temperature or light absorption characteristic. This new color, the one to which they are evolving, when it is achieved, may bring about other changes like changes in composition, temperature, and the like. There may be a hundred scientific explanations for this change, but I don't know any. That's why I sent the scanned images and my notes to several of my international colleagues. I anticipate hearing from them very soon, despite the significant time differences, because I marked the e-mail Urgent/Max Priority."

"This is *ferclanicht*. Crazy. Stones that feel. Stones that break the laws of nature and physical science. Stones that grow and change like plants or people. Professor, have you spoken to the stones today? Have they answered? What's next? A little song and dance routine?"

Michael has never seen his father so upset. His voice is forceful yet quivering, as if he is holding back anger or fear. He is straining. His hands are flat on the table, pushing down so hard the knuckles are white.

"Boys, listen to what this so-called professor is saying. He is telling us these are not stones… they are freaks of nature with animate properties. That as we all know is impossible. And, I am embarrassed for you, Father, and you, Pastor Zug. You sought the aid of a stranger and he has given you what you want. The man of science comes to our valley and tells you just enough, adds the right embroidery, to make you believe in the supernatural. Yet to be told is his cure-all for what ails you. A few bottles of Doctor Tomas' magic elixir, for a very steep price, will solve your problems and make this craziness go away. Father. Amos. How could you let yourselves be hoodwinked like this? Or maybe you wanted to be tricked, because if an expert confirms your fantasies, they must be real. If they are real, you are special. I am very disappointed in both of you. And I'm upset that you snookered my son into your merry band of illogic. Starting now, that is over. Michael and Aaron are forbidden to have anything to do with this whole insanity. Father, as their grandfather, I implore you to Keep the boys far away from this *ferclanicht* mess. And, I beg you, as your son, to separate yourself from these two men. Pastor Amos, you're on your own. But, understand that we can no longer come to your church. In fact, if this insanity continues I will be required to discuss the matter with the congregation and recommend your removal. Boys, let's go home. Father, I suggest you do the same. Come with us or walk, it's your choice."

"Ruben, you're acting foolish. I think the professor has uncovered a great mystery that will explain all that has been going on in the valley. His discoveries and observations about the stones are beginning to make sense to me. And to Michael. There are many things in the everyday world, which we pass over because we don't see or recognize them. Stones are like that. Also, there can be things about the ordinary that are not ordinary. The professor believes, and I do too, that these stones are like that. He has asked for help from other professors to give him their opinion about the stones. I want to see that. Then we'll proceed. The pastor is a man of God. He believes in God. He has faith in God. He also believes in evil. Maybe that's Satan. Maybe it's just people, who don't follow the will of God. I don't know, but Pastor Zug knows evil has existed since before man and it exists today. Who's to say it's not the same evil? Just as it is the same God. Just suppose for a moment that these stones are foretelling a cataclysmic event. Foretelling in little events a great event to come. Suppose the evil that dwells in the Tal is just giving us a hint of the destruction it will rain upon us. Then, this evil must be dealt with. Disposed of, before it can cause any more damage to the farm, the livestock, or destroy us."

"Listen to yourself and your prattle. This evil, as you call it, is tipping its hand, and giving us hints so that we can confront it and crush it. Why the hints? Why not a full-scale attack? Is the evil flirting with us? Or, is it so stupid to think that we won't do anything about it? Or, better still, is the evil conning us into thinking we can fight it? Trapping us so it can crush us before we run away. And, where, in God's name, would we run to from such an all-powerful evil? Do you honestly think that we, as mere mortals, have the power to overcome an evil force that can kill and gut a Guernsey, cause buzzards to attack before dawn, and mutilate our dogs and leave no trace? David and Goliath are characters in a story in the bible. Their story, like all the stories in the bible, is a myth. The truth of the matter is that there is no sinister force. The recent events are aberrations of nature. We are not under the threat of destruction. We…that is, you two, are under the threat of a huge hoax. My boys and I will not sit in the company of fools and be swayed by old wives' tales of shadows in the night. Boys, we are leaving. Now."

Michael looks at his father then Neen. The boy wants to stay and be part of the adventure, but he must obey his father. Even Neen would want it that way. Aaron rises slowly, glaring at the older men. His bravado is built solely upon his father's righteous indignation.

"You know what I think? I think this professor guy has put you under his spell. You come running to him with a dark puzzle. He knows what you want to hear, so he tells you. Then he claims to be sending the material and his notes to people all over the world. Do you know that for sure? Maybe he is just sending the computer stuff to a confederate in Montana, or wherever he claims to be from. This confederate will confirm just enough information to push the exploration further and to gain your confidence completely. He will leave enough open to interpretation to allow Pastor Zug and grandfather to discover new and confirming truths. It's like a magician and his assistant. It's a very elaborate con. Neen, be careful, the professor will probably ask you for money or the deed to the farm. He will need the money for some special ray gun or atomic blasting caps to destroy the Tal. Michael, you're young and naive. You're easily swayed by Neen and the pastor. That's why you have to listen to Dad and me now. We want only what's best for you. Let's go home."

Aaron's parroting of Ruben's point-of-view hurts Michael. Aaron rarely thinks for himself. He usually follows the loudest or last speaker, and tonight that speaker is Ruben. Michael's resolve hardens.

Father and sons head for the door in silence. They never look back.

"Isaac, I'm sorry this is causing a rift in your family. I would wish that not to happen. If you want to go with them, Vincent and I will understand."

"No. But, thank you Amos. I'm old enough to make up my own mind on all matters. If Ruben and his boys don't agree, so be it. That will not stop me from doing what I think is right. Vincent, can we do anything but wait?"

"Let's look at the family bible."

The big book is opened on the table. Amos paces.

DRAGON SLAYER

"Hello Mrs. Hess. Is Michael around?"

"Good evening, Jimmy. Yes. He's upstairs in his room. You're welcome to go up."

"Thanks."

"Michael, watcha doin'?"

"Nothing much. Just reading a magazine on fishing."

"You've gotta come with me."

"Why?"

"Mary Ruth needs your help."

"What kind of help? And, how come you're tellin' me and not her?"

"She's in the truck outside waitin' for you and me to come and help her."

"Help her?"

"Yeah, she came over to my place and she was all cryin' and complainin'. She looked like she had been in a fight. Her clothes were torn and everything. That's when she asked me to bring her here. She said you'd help her."

Michael has his shoes on and is halfway down the stairs in two heartbeats.

"Mom. Dad. Is it OK if I go out with Jimmy Hauck for a while? We're just gonna' drive over to the Millersville Diner. Jimmy's got his dad's truck. I'll be home by eleven. OK?"

Generation before and generations to come. The child seeks permission as he is headed out the door. Parents assent, because they cannot stop this rite of passage.

"What happened to you?"

"Gene Dracal pushed me around and I got real scared and went to Jimmy's cause it was close and I asked him to bring me here 'cause I knew you'd know what to do 'cause I'm still scared of those people I'm afraid they might do something to me."

"It's OK, Mary Ruth, you're safe now. Stop crying and slow down. Give me all the details. Then we'll decide what to do."

"You need to go over to Gene Dracal's house and deal with him right now. He slapped me, pushed me down, and tore my clothes."

"You need to explain to me exactly what happened. Then we need to discuss what we should or can do about it."

"OK."

Her sigh of resignation was an exhale before the verbal assault on her evening's enemies.

"Well, a group of us were invited over to Gene's for a party. There was Gwen, Margaret, Louisa, Jeannie, Mary Beth, and me. We took two cars... Louisa's and Mary Beth's. When we got to Gene's, we knew they had been drinking. I mean out by the pool, there were beer cans all over and a few Vodka bottles on the tables. There must have been twenty other people. The usual crowd of guys that hangs around Gene... Butch, Jimmy, Boyd, Jack, Billy, the whole gang was there. Plus, they had invited a bunch of kids from other schools. Some girls from Country Day School and some guys from McCaskey. Like I said, the pool area was crowded. Some kids were swimming, some just sitting listening to really loud music, and some were dancin'. Gene and a few of his buddies were smokin'. And I don't mean cigarettes. I sat down to talk to a few of the kids. They offered me a beer. Gwen had one, so did Louisa. So I figured what the heck. I took the beer. Then we all started dancin'. Just a large group bouncin' at poolside. No couples. The boys passed around some more beers. Then the craziest thing. A couple of the kids jumped in the pool, clothes and all. Then a couple more. Two guys took off their clothes and were skinny-dipping. Two girls from Country Day took off their tops and shorts. Kept the panties on and they were sort of skinny-dipping. With all the lights in the pool, you could see everything. At this time, Jeannie and I were standing on the side of the pool. All of a sudden, Gene pushed me from behind. I flopped into the pool. Then he jumped in nearly on top of me. He grabbed me and tried to kiss me. Then he tried to pull down my shorts. I think that's when he tore my top. I panicked and slapped him. And I started to scream. Then he held me underwater, all the while tugging at my clothes. When he let me up, I punched and kicked him. I think I hit him in the nose, 'cause there was blood in the water. He grabbed my hair and pulled me to the side of the pool. Then he climbed out and yanked me up to the patio. He dragged me over the flagstone to the grass and he pushed me down. Before he could climb on top of me, I kicked him and scrambled away around the house to the cars. That's when it dawned on me that I had to find my own way home. But, that was too far. I knew Jimmy's house was just over the hill. I could run that. I asked Jimmy to bring me here."

"Michael, we have to do something."

"Yes Michael, you have to do something to Gene and his bunch of thugs."

"Let me think."

"Think about what? Gene Dracal nearly raped me, and you want to think."

"Jimmy, drive over to Gene's. I want to talk to him."

"Just talk? After what he did to me, you just want to talk?"

"It's the only place to start."

Except for road noise, the trip is quiet. The smell of beer is strong in the cab even with the windows open. The Dracals live on the old Darmstetter farm. Forty acres of prime land with its own water source, a huge stable, complete riding and jumping grounds, and six of the most beautiful thoroughbreds in the county. Dr. Dracal was retired from the medical profession before the family moved here. Mrs. Dracal is twenty-five years younger than her husband and is rumored to be sweet on the horse trainer. The Dracals are always out of town for one thing and another. Gene is tended by the cook and yardman. The driveway to the house is a semi-circular lane about a half-mile long. In front of the house it looks like the parking lot for the rich and famous of the county. Jimmy's truck is the only one.

"Both of you stay here while I go and talk to Gene. I'm sure I can handle this alone and there is no need for further violence. I'll only be a few minutes. Please stay here."

"Michael, I'm coming with you. You'll be outnumbered. I can cover your back."

"If both of us go in there to talk to Gene, he'll assume we're looking to fight him. I don't want to fight. I want no violence. I want a resolution to this matter and for him to understand that his actions are not acceptable."

"Michael, look, Daniel had to go into the lion's den. You have a choice. Let me just walk in there with you. It's like we heard of the party and hoped they wouldn't be upset if we invited ourselves."

"They know already I'm not a party boy. That's why I wasn't invited. Gene knows how I feel about Mary Ruth. That's why my showing up here will be no surprise to him. Your arrival will set off the alarms, so please stay here. I'll handle it peacefully. I need you to stay here and keep Mary Ruth company. Most of all I need you to be ready to leave in a hurry. If things don't go as I hope in there, I may come running around the corner. Then we should leave right away. OK?"

"OK."

"Be careful, Michael. I don't want you to get hurt."

"I don't want that either."

Michael doesn't bother to get to the pool through the house. He walks on the path around the left side of the building. The noises, which are audible from Jimmy's truck, become pulsing with nearness. Despite its volume, the music can't drown the shrieks, laughter, and screams of the pool splashers. The sight is, to the boy of simple exposure, debauchery. Girls and boys: some naked and some with just underwear. Wet underwear that reveals all. Beside the pool there is extensive kissing and groping. He is stunned into inertia.

"Hey, Gene, we have a guest. Mikey the milker. What the hell are you doing here farm boy?"

"Billy, I'll bet he wants to grow up. Ya' know, drink some beer, smoke some dope, and get laid."

"Gene, I'd like to talk to you."

"I'm here milker. Just speak up. The fun of life is drowning out your naive whispers."

"I'd like to talk to you in private."

"I can talk to you and still fool around. Did you ever fool around milker?"

"I'd hoped we could deal with this alone."

"There is nothing you can say to me that you can't say to all my friends. Look at these tits, milker. Ever see anything so firm and warm that wasn't attached to a Guernsey? By the way how are your Guernseys? And your dogs?"

"I'll ask again. Can we talk somewhere without all these people?"

"No, but because I am a great guy, I'll have the sound turned way down so you can speak your piece before you leave."

"Gene, leave the sound alone, it's just gettin' good."

"Relax, Jack, snuggle up to Gwen for a second, while I listen to Mikey. Here, Mikey, sit with me at my table."

All eyes were on the pair as they settled at the table.

"Now tell me why you had the balls to barge into my party."

"I came here at the request of Mary Ruth Martin. She told me that you were rude and abusive to her earlier this evening. She is upset and I want to fully understand what happened."

"What happened is quite simple. She came on to me. She kissed me and was rubbing my crotch. She pushed me in the water and started to pull off my pants. She obviously wanted the weasel. I wasn't interested in her. I never have been interested in her. She is a cock teaser. She comes on to all the guys, and then backs off at the moment of truth. Her friends will tell you the truth. Look around you. See familiar faces and chests. Ask any one of them. Mary Ruth became pissed when I rejected her. She got violent. She punched me in the nose. Look, it's bruised. I had to defend myself. I pushed her away real hard. She became hysterical crying. She ran off into the night. The last thing I heard from her was that she was going to get me. So, I don't know what she told you, but I'll bet it's a lie. The little cock teaser is a big liar."

Michael looks at Louisa and then Jeannie. Both look away. No one will defend Mary Ruth. The boy knows it's pointless to ask any of the guys from school. They'll lie to protect their host.

"That's not true. That's not how it went."

Margaret's delicate voice cut the warm silence like a klaxon.

"Well, Maggie the whore, what do you have to add? One sleazy bitch defends another. Boy, that's rich. I'm surprised you can even speak. I mean being so close to Billy's crotch and all."

"How did it happen, Maggie?"

"Michael, we came here for the party. Things got out of hand too quickly.

71

Beer, smoke, and music. The pool. It started out as fun, but it became something different in a hurry. Gene grabbed Mary Ruth. Not the way he says. He pushed her in the pool and jumped on top of her. She had to fight to get away. He pawed her in the pool and on the grass. She ran."

"Well, there it is milker. Who are you going to believe? Two sleazy whores or me?"

As he is reviewing the situation, Michael realizes there is someone behind him. Before he can speak, he feels the blow to his shoulder. The pain is numbing. He gasps for breath and teeters to the table. Before a second blow can be administered, Michael ducks and reaches up to grab Gene's throat with his right hand. He pinches his thumb and forefinger around the boy's windpipe. Gene's eyes bulge in panic. Michael stands up and walks this new appendage to the grass, all the while attempting to get his thumb and index finger to meet inside Gene's throat. Gene follows obediently and bellows in a raspy tenor.

"Jesus, fucking Christ, do something before he kills me. He's as crazy as his bitch."

Billy tackles the odd couple and the three tumble to the ground. Neen had told Michael to end a fight before it begins. This grip will do that. The absence of oxygen has a debilitating effect on the desire to fight. Once applied, the grip is not to be loosened until the opponent yields. It is that simple. As long as Michael maintains his grip, he is in control. And he must be willing and able to sustain attacks from others to hold the grip. He is holding on for his own life.

Butch is next to hit Michael. He uses a small piece of wood. The blow glances off Michael's left shoulder blade. He can feel the pain down to his knees. Boyd and Jimmy hit Michael with filled quart bottles of beer. They bounce off Michael and shatter on the pool deck. Gene's eyes reflect real fear. He can feel the life of breath extinguished. He tries to loosen the grip. Then, as Neen had instructed, Michael hits Gene's ribs with his left fist using all the strength he can muster. Gene exhales. Now there is no air in his lungs and none coming in. The mask of near death covers Gene Dracal. Jack hits Michael's right elbow downward and the vise is open. Michael falls to the deck and rolls into a tight fetal position. Thereafter, the partygoers use Michael as a piñata, striking him from all sides and with all manner of fist, foot, and stick. He doesn't clearly hear the gun's report. He vaguely feels Jimmy picking him up and putting him in the truck cab. He never sees Jimmy wipe the fluid from his hands.

"Wrap his head in my shirt. My dad doesn't need to know about Michael's battle wounds. We can't take him home like this. We've got to tend to his wounds. We can't take him to my place. My folks are home. What about yours?"

"My folks went over to see my sister. They won't be home until around midnight. Maybe we should take him to the emergency ward instead. The injuries could be serious."

"No hospital. They'll ask questions, and fill out forms, then the police will be called, and we'll have to explain why we went there. Then they'll have to investigate what was going on there. A lot of parents will be called and a lot of questions will be asked. Are you ready to explain to the police? No, my way is the better way. We get Michael to your place, do a temporary fix, and get him home. We'll need to have the same story as to how he got the cuts and bruises."

By the time Jimmy gets to the Martin house, Michael is conscious. His eyes are open and he is trying to move his fingers, hands, and arms. The pain has numbed his body.

"Just be still while we wash you off and check out your wounds. Take him to my bathroom, get him undressed and into a shower. Lots of soap and shampoo. Got to get the glass off. Wash him down real good."

Removing Michael's shirt and pants reveals many red welts that will be bruises tomorrow. The stiffness and soreness will be intense. Not too many cuts, except small ones on his arms, head, and shoulders.

"Michael, do you understand me when I speak?"

"Jimmy, no need to yell. I'm not deaf. I understand you completely. I need you to wash my clothes. Now you can leave me alone."

The cleansing process is slow and painful. Muscles are bruised and shards of glass scrape Michael's flesh on their way down the drain. It all happened so quickly he can't recall the details. Finally he emerges from the bathroom, one towel around his waist and one over his shoulders.

"You're going to have to sit in the chair while I put medicine on your cuts. I can't do anything about the welts, but you can't go home looking like you were with people who didn't care about you. I'll be as gentle as I can, but it's going to sting."

"What are you going to put on me?"

"I'm going to wash the cuts with hydrogen peroxide to flush out any debris you missed in the shower. Then I'm going to apply some antibiotic ointment to prevent infection. A few of the scrapes are deep and a few are wide. I'll put bandages on them. But, most are too small for a bandage or even a Band-Aid. While I'm nursing to you, we'll have to come up with some explanation for your condition."

Except for the pain, the administration is sensuous. Mary Ruth's delicate and caring fingers glide over Michael's flesh. They pause at the appropriate places and daub a soaked cotton ball on the cuts. After the hydrogen peroxide's bubbling, the ointment lovingly covers the flesh opening. If a bandage is needed, gauze is laid tenderly over the tended spot and tape is applied at two ends. A few times Michael feels his nurse stroke the back of his neck up to his skull. She claims to be searching for glass.

"There, noble warrior, your wounds are taken care of. In a few days you'll be back to full health. Jimmy, where are his clothes?"

"I'll bring them up in ten minutes. He'll just have to wait. I'd say keep his pants on but that would be impossible."

The nurse is standing in front of the patient.

"I forgot to check your face and chest for cuts and scrapes."

Her fingers trace small lines and circles over Michael's forehead, eyelids, ears, nose, lips, and chin. They seem to skip down his neck to his chest. With his eyes closed, he can't see her expression or how close to his face is her mouth. The touch of her lips upon his causes his eyes to pop open and all of his body to stiffen.

"What are you doing?"

"Do you like it?"

"Yes, I like it. But, Jimmy will be up here any minute. He could catch us."

"Catch us doing what?"

"Kissing."

Her lips are now about a quarter inch away from his and her warm hands are on his waist. He can feel her fingers sneaking between the towel and his flesh. Then her tongue slithers into his open mouth. It runs along his lips leaving moisture and skips across his teeth creating dryness. Darting in and out. Twitching and flickering. He feels light headed and warm all over.

"Here I come. I hope you're both decent. No fooling around between nurse and patient. I got the solution to our not-the real-story problem. The clothes are a little damp and quite hot, but they'll be dry by the time you get home. Put them on then we'll talk."

"What is this masterful lie to which we must swear?"

"It's so simple. You fell out of the truck as we were leaving the diner. You thought the door was shut tight, but as we turned onto the road, the door popped open and out you plopped. The rest is the truth. We got you back here and Nurse Martin brought you back to life with washes, ointments, and loving care. The entire evening and all of your cuts and bruises are explained away. Is that perfect or what?"

"Then we'll have to go to the diner so they can see us."

"Brilliant addition, nurse. Is the patient able to travel?"

"I am."

The sloppy ice cream treats are suitable rewards for their escapade. Not too far away, over toward the river, they can hear the sirens of the police and fire departments. No flames on the horizon. The problem can't be too big. To confirm the story, they would need to roar away from the diner. This is Jimmy's shining moment. All the other teens in their cars and trucks look in awe as the rear wheels kick up dust and stones and then screech on to the black top. The lines of rubber are twenty feet in first gear and punctuated with a hard shift into second and another three feet of Goodyear's finest.

"That will let everyone know we were there. Now to get you home before the bewitching hour of eleven."

The lights are out at the Hess farm. There will be no questions. Michael's sleep is fitful. The discomfort of physical pain is heightened by thoughts of the evening with the pastor and professor. Michaels frets how his father abandoned him.

The sun pierces the bedroom window blinds and the boy's eyelids. He hears his mother calling from far away.

"Michael, it's time to get up for church."

Arising is excruciating. Michael's back, ribs, and shoulders feel as if he has to stretch them to fit his body. The flesh that holds the bruised bones has contracted and hardened in a natural reflex. He has to loosen the wrap to become mobile. Every movement hurts. And, not just the first time. The pain sears each and every time. No time to shower. He needs all the time to get dressed.

"What happened to you? Are you all right? Ruben, do you think we should get him to the hospital?"

"Michael, what happened?"

The rehearsed story is accepted as gospel.

"*Doplick.*"

"Aaron, be kind to Michael. He fell and he's hurt."

"Let's get going to church and thank God nothing worse happened to you, and that you have such a good friend as Mary Ruth."

Sitting upright on the hard pew is more than uncomfortable. It is torture. The bruises in Michael's buttocks and hips stimulate foggy memories of last night's events. The sermon deals with messages and signs of both good and evil that are all around us every day. A few we see and understand, but most we don't until it's too late. There is a constant battle between God and Satan for our souls. This war is all around us all the time. And, we are more than passive participants, we are soldiers. Because we have free will, we can choose to fight in a righteous manner or we can fall under the spell of the Great Dragon. We can fight against the temptations of the Beast; the seductions of opulence, of lust, and of greed. These are sins that separate us from the will of God. And separation from God is the ultimate sin, because it means the Devil has our soul.

Lust is the worst sin of all, because it is based on abusive power. We seek power over another human. The person, for whom we lust, becomes an object. This other loses all form of humanity. There is no equality or tenderness. When we lust, we abandon our divine characteristics and take on the mantle of the animals. When we lust, we do not love, but we fornicate. There is only the vicious desire to satisfy our lust. Lust wells up within us and twists us into ugly beasts. When our lust is satisfied, we abandon the object. We do not cleave to the other person as a loved one. Our momentary need has been satisfied, so we move on to conquer another. In a world filled with lust, we must strive to love. Be tender, be merciful, be understanding of the feelings of the other. Pastor Zug is on fire. He is waving his arms and nearly shouting. Sweat beads on his face. Despite the occasional babbling and rambling Michael feels the man makes some sense. The collection plate is piled high. The closing hymn is boisterous. Standing feels better than sitting, and much better than walking.

"Today you get to be babied, my baby. After breakfast, I want you to sit deep in a hot tub for as long as you can. That will loosen the bruises. And take aspirin every four hours. Now let's all have a nice Sunday breakfast, read the paper and share our thoughts and feelings about today's sermon."

Sunday breakfast consists of slab bacon, three kinds of sausage, scrapple, fried eggs, pancakes, muffins with honey and fresh fruit. Everyone in the family except Michael helps so it would be easier on mother. There will be no evening meal. Every Sunday, the family is encouraged to raid the refrigerator whenever they want something to eat. Nothing for mother to do except be waited on.

"Look at this on the front page."

Car crash kills six teens.

Eugene Dracal, Wendell Reyfsnyder, James Leonard, Boyd Wenton, Elmer Messersmith, and William Stowe died in a fiery auto accident on Hunsecker Mill Road beside the Conestoga River. The accident occurred at approximately 10 PM when Eugene Dracal apparently lost control of the automobile as he was attempting to negotiate the turns and unevenness of the old farm road. The youth was unable to control the expensive European sedan. The sedan, travelling at a high rate of speed apparently careened off the embankment on the side of the Zook farm. The car then flipped completely over and roared unimpeded over the next four hundred yards. There were no tire marks immediately before the car crashed into a huge rock extrusion at the river's side. All six boys perished in the fire. The police have opened an investigation into this accident. There were no more details available at press time.

PASTOR

Wednesday there will be no chores. Michael, Jimmy, and Mary Ruth are going to funeral services. The first will be at St. Stephen's Episcopal Church for five of the boys killed in the accident. Then, Dr. and Mrs. Dracal are having a non-church event at their home for Gene.

St. Stephen's is a very high Episcopal Church. Incense and a little Latin are part of each service. The kids call it Smokey Steve's. The church has a deep tradition within the county, state, and the country. Several signers of the Declaration of Independence were members and are buried in the cemetery. Governors, senators, and all sorts of the business powerful were and are members of St. Stephen's. Parking close to the church is impossible. Michael's classmates and their parents shuffle through the huge double oak doors and find whatever seating they can. The light within the church comes through the windows and is supplemented by hundreds of candles. Five urns stand on the altar as testimony of today's purpose.

The stained glass windows cascade beautiful hues of light across the body of the building and the people in attendance. Windows depict important events in the life of Christ, the disciples, and the growth of Christianity. In the walls to the right and left of the altar, Michael notices scenes different from the rest. There are no recognizable people. One wall contains a window showing some sort of mass confusion. Storm clouds and lightning surround loosely shaped human-like forms. Fallen shapes and frozen activity give the appearance of a battle. There are no faces, as there are on the other windows. Only hints of features. One side of the mêlée is winning or at least pressing forward. They are in white tunics, each with a radiant gold star on the front. Their swords and armor are also golden. Their enemy seems similarly uniformed and equipped, except the star doesn't radiate and their armor is gray. The side with the advantage seems to be pushing the other side to the edge of the window.

On the other wall, the window illustrates the apparent victors basking in a great light in the clouds. The vanquished have been reduced in size and number, and are standing on some surface well below the victors. The defeated seem to be waving their weapons at the others. The impression of great anger is depicted in the contrast between the orange and yellow jagged lines, the dark colors and ill-shapen forms. Brown and very dark blue dominate. Staring at what should be their faces; Michael sees they seem to be yelling at the shapes above. The two windows grip the boy's attention. Religion is often so violent on earth, because the struggle is for eternity. Despite the violence of the two windows, he is at peace in these surroundings. As the service begins, he notices that the church is filled to capacity. Jimmy and Mary Ruth are fidgeting. Their eyes dart as if they are frightened.

The opening hymn is *Amazing Grace*. The priest reads from the Burial Service. One by one each of the parents of the five boys comes to the lectern and speaks about his or her son and what will be missed. They were good children, who didn't deserve to die this way. Michael asks himself: What way would have been appropriate for them to die before old age? Michael is sad that his classmates are dead, but they died as they lived: wild and with regard only for a godless life. Nothing can change that. God will forgive them for they are children. Mercifully, the service is over at noon. The Dracals have invited only children to their house at one.

"That was spooky. The windows and the candles. The whole place smelled old, like my grandmother's house. Really old."

"I don't think it was spooky. I think it was peaceful. Regardless of how they lived, the boys' souls are at peace now."

"Mary Ruth is right. All that mumbo jumbo about soul and God's great love. The guys died. Their bodies burned. Too much was made of God's will. If he is so good and so powerful, why didn't he prevent the deaths? Why did he will them to die? Why not a big accident with injuries? Why not nothing at all? If he can't do that, how does he expect us to think of him as all-powerful?

If he is not all-powerful, why should we care about him? God is God and humans are humans. And never the twain shall meet."

Sarah Miller walks the short path from the church parking lot to Amos Zug's house. She lets herself in and goes directly to the office and her administrative duties for the church. She has been working part time for Amos and the church for a year. The confusion on the desk is more intense than normal, due to Amos' late nights with Vincent. She begins by sorting and stacking piles of papers and open books.

"Sarah, is that you?"

"Yes, Pastor."

"I'm sorry the office is such a mess. I'll be down to help you in a few minutes. In the meantime, would you make the coffee?"

"Yes."

As the machine is in the throws of perking, she hears Amos' footsteps on the stairs. It is after noon. His lax work habits are more pronounced these days. Ever since they started his little game, he has become self-absorbed. He wasn't always this way. As she opens the mail, she senses him in the doorway and turns to greet him.

"Good day, Pastor."

"When you are here, I'm Amos and you're Sarah."

"Amos, I'll open your mail, so you can read it while I get these papers categorized and organized. Is that all right with you?"

"That will be fine. Have you had lunch, or shall I prepare something for both of us?"

"Thank you, but I've eaten."

She can't help but notice he is casually dressed. Not like a pastor. Pull over golf shirt, khakis, and loafers without socks. And he has put on heavy, sweet cologne. Did he bathe in it? As always he is staring back at her. The game has officially begun.

The Dracal driveway is lined on both sides with cars and pick up trucks. As Jimmy and his passengers crunch their way to the entrance, they are joined by several others, who had been at the church service. The double doors are open and classmates are milling in the hall as if waiting for something to happen.

"Do you get the feeling we are in the camp of the enemy?"

"Michael, how could you? Gene is dead. We'll pay our respects to his parents and leave if you're nervous."

"I'm not nervous. It's just that the last time we were here was the last time we saw Gene and his buddies alive. The night Gene and I fought. I get the strange feeling I could be blamed for what happened."

"Don't be stupid. You were in no shape to harm anybody. By the time we got you into the truck, you were lucky to be alive. How could you have known Gene and his buddies would go joy riding after we left?"

"You're right. It's crazy."

"Dr. Dracal, I'm Mary Ruth Martin. I'm very sorry about Gene."

"Thank you. You must be Michael Hess."

"Yessir, and this is Jimmy Hauck."

"Michael, this is my wife, Angelica."

"Pleased to meet you, Mrs. Dracal. I'm sorry our meeting has to be under such unfortunate circumstances."

"Yes. Help yourself to some refreshments. The food and beverages are in the dining room. We will have a brief ceremony in about fifteen minutes."

Michael and Mary Ruth get in line for canapés and punch, while Jimmy wanders off.

"You guys, you got to see the library."

At the end of a narrow hall off the living room is an archway with an ornately carved black door. Almost invisible in the shadows are two gargoyles perched above the entrance. The brass door handle works silently. Six eyes peer inside.

"Michael, have you ever seen a room like this; a library with no lights or windows? Only candles for light. And the books look older than your family bible. There must be a thousand. Behind the desk, there's a painting. I can't make out what it's about, can you? This room is too weird for words."

"Jimmy, we have no business prying into their private lives. It's bad enough they lost their son, but for us to be spying, that's insult to injury."

"Mary Ruth, you're such a goodie two shoes."

"She's right we must get out of here immediately. It's too private and I feel something is not right here. We do not belong."

"Come here you two. Look at the painting. What is that? Is it a battle? It looks like a snake attacking a building. I think I can see people in windows and the yard within the building."

"It's a dragon. In ancient times, superstitious people believed that dragons roamed the earth. These dragons were threats to the people's temporal power. People believed they had to destroy all the dragons before the land would be truly safe. Of course, this was all just silly superstition. There were no dragons, only ignorance and xenophobia, the fear of others. All others were perceived as threats to the lives of every tribe or clan that thought it was a nation. Harmony was not possible because of irrational fear. Fear fostered by those who sought to maintain power and control over each tribe. The leaders were shamans who kept their people in line with myths and lies. The others, the outsiders, wanted only to live in the peace of equality. But, the tribe's ruling fathers, fearing the loss of authority, would have none of that. So those in authority created the dragon and the people associated with the dragon were persecuted. There were great battles, so called between good and evil, and thousands were slaughtered. Lives wasted for the protection of personal power. Denial of equality based on fear produces conflict. Now will you join the rest of your classmates poolside?"

Dr. Dracal's history lesson sends chills over the three. He takes a book from his desk.

Engrossed in the disheveled mass of papers on the desk, Sarah is oblivious to Amos' approach from behind. But, his cologne precedes him. Except for her hands, she does not move. Not frozen in fear, but resigned to the unfolding of predetermined events. Gently his hands rest on her shoulders. He lowers his face to the left side of her neck and begins to trace his lips from her shoulder to her ear. She stares at the wall knowing what actions and words will follow.

"I count the hours until the time you're here. Three days a week is not enough. I'm less than half full when you're not with me. And, I overflow with joy when you and I are one. I want to sweep you up and be inside of you so we can be one forever."

His hands creep to the buttons on her blouse and initiate the undressing ritual. His breaths are deep and fluttering. Moisture from his breath and his spit spill onto her back. He inserts his hand in her blouse. Sarah does not wear a bra on these days. His fingers massage the orbs. Then index fingers and thumbs roll her nipples. She reflexively squirms on the chair. Her hands drop to her sides, reach behind the chair, and grasp his thighs…then buttocks. This excites real urgency to his massaging. On cue, she rises and turns to accept the mouth and tongue of her provocateur. Four hands now compete for the honor of victory: who can undress whom first. Papers are strewn on the floor by her blouse, forcibly removed and tossed. Sarah has unhooked Amos' belt and pants clasp. In the process of removing his pants, Amos tears the zipper. The activity is frenzied. Mouths are locked then unlocked as tongues explore chests, arms, and stomachs. Tugging furiously on her skirt, Amos discards it in the office corner. He throws her onto the desk and hoists her legs. The pull on Sarah's panties is so strong as to cause red marks on the outside of her thighs. He dives on her and proceeds to rub his spittle on every inch of her flesh and into every opening from scalp to navel.

He pulls her down so her feet touch the floor, and devours her the way no other woman ever allowed. His paroxysms of joy are faint, but she senses them nonetheless and rolls her over to her stomach. This is what Amos wants. This is what Amos must have. He must dominate so he can feel complete. He must brutalize. Fortunately, the discomfort won't last long. She seizes the sides of the desk to absorb his entry blow. Feral instincts rule. The initial thrust is shallow and it stings. The second thrust is only slightly deeper and less painful. Sarah struggles to keep her feet on the floor and yet be in position to receive and increase Amos' lust. She does not look to her fornicator. Once she looked upon him, and she saw only deep torment. The strange mixture of lust and shame contorted his face. She can feel him all over as he mercilessly squeezes her hips and buttocks. He pulls her hair in an attempt to force his type of pleasure upon her. She feels none. Amos whimpers as his pumping reaches a frantic rhythm. She arches back to ease her discomfort. He bites her shoulder. She tries to bury her chest in the desktop to escape further pain. Suddenly he freezes. His breath is that of someone suffering an asthma attack. As is their custom, Sarah continues to gyrate and his spasms begin. Wave after luxuriating wave, the pulses of joy rush from toe to ear. Twisting Amos' spinal column. His shoulders tremble and he withdraws. He is through. Sarah can relax, because her ordeal is over.

"Dr. Dracal and I thank you for coming to Gene's memorial service. We view this as a testimony of your respect and love of him. Now my husband would like to say a few words."

"Ladies. Gentlemen. There will be no prayers today. Only a brief reading from the book of ancient letters. The one I chose for today is from a father to his son who is a general at war far away. The irony is that the old man does not know that his son has already been killed. Not by the enemy, but the boy has been killed by his own men before the battle commenced. A mutiny among captains and lieutenants killed the son. Nonetheless, the father writes, hoping the young man will read the epistle before he enjoins the perceived enemy."

Light of my life, I wish you well. I wish that you be victorious in this battle and in all battles to come. I pray that you remain strong and true to the cause of your kingdom. Your kingdom, because it will be so upon my departure to the land of rest. You are about to embark upon a great battle from which you will return victorious. You will vanquish the evil outsider, who tries to chain us like slaves. Slavery is not possible to those who know the freedom of equality. I want you to hold within your breastplate the lessons of freedom and equality, and what must be accomplished to maintain these precious ideas. These you must pass on to your children and their children. For freedom is sustained only through vigilance and struggle. My heart is filled with admiration for you. I remember you as a child, a youth, and now a leader. Fight with the fire of hundreds and return to the safety of your home and family.

"This is how Mrs. Dracal and I will remember my son. The spark of his life will never dim in our hearts. We know Gene is doing what he loves most. We know he is living on another plane…another dimension. As I live, I will see his soul in many things. Here at his home and throughout the land. That is the power of my love."

The doctor is holding an urn with handles and elaborate metal work, totally different from the urns at St. Stephens. He carries it to the paddock fence. Standing against the fence, he removes the urn's lid, and begins to chant. Michael can't distinguish the words, but they sound vaguely like those in his family's bible. Then with a single sweep of his arm and hand, the contents of the urn are sent windward. The dust travels and disperses until it is no longer visible. The doctor turns to face the attendees and intones:

"He is."

Michael does not realize Mrs. Dracal is standing so close behind him, almost touching him. She is dressed completely in black, and a gossamer veil hides her face.

"Michael, Gene always spoke well of you. I hope you will think well of him in his absence."

"Mrs. Dracal, Gene will be missed by his classmates, particularly those of us who knew him well. I know Jimmy Hauck and Mary Ruth Martin will miss him, too. Have you spoken to them?"

"No I haven't. I'm sure I will before they leave. My husband tells me you are interested in our library. He and Gene were particularly proud of the truth and wisdom sheltered in that room. Would you like me to take you to the library?"

Post coitus is such an awkward time. The searing heat and blinding steam of Amos' lust have been vanquished by the release of visceral tension, and replaced by the unsociable states of nakedness and small talk. Bodily hygiene is optional. Today papers have to be rearranged and a work place put in proper order. Clothes are the last items of attention. No one ever visits Amos. She has work to do.

"After I take care of the office, I guess I should start gathering a file for the newsletter"

"I love you."

"Amos, get real. You don't love me. You love what we do together. I like it too, but I don't love you."

"That's not true. I love you and you love me."

"Now you're being silly. Like a little boy."

"If you don't love me, why do you do this with me?"

"I like it. It gives me pleasure, I make money, and it's safe. I mean, I hope this was as much as would come of our relationship. I get paid because you get laid. Where else am I going to earn $300 for three short days of work? What could be bad? I don't talk. You don't talk. Nobody knows. Not my folks. Not the congregation. Not Aaron. You and I keep these fun times quiet as long as we want them to go on."

"You harlot."

"If I'm a harlot, what are you? You are a hypocritical, deceitful, fallen man of the cloth. Whom do you think the congregation and the public will consider most evil, a woman forced into carnal knowledge by her religious beacon or the beacon, who forced her? Who gets the sympathy here and who gets crucified?"

"What are you saying?"

"I'm saying, if you're going to behave like a teenager and ignore the reality of the situation, it's time we go our separate ways. Besides, the limitation to our relationship is annoying. We can't go anywhere but here and we can't do anything but screw. Where is our life? When I say life, I'm looking ahead. When you say life, you are trying to remember. I want out of this so I can move on with my life, now."

"What do you mean?"

"I mean that I'm done coming over here so you can get your jollies. I mean I'm tired of my singular role in your life. The money just isn't worth the emotional aggravation. I mean I quit. When I walk out that door, I'll never return. You can send the check to my house. When we see each other again, it will be as if we never did any of this."

"You can't leave me. What will I do without you?"

"Find someone else to screw or take matters into your own hand."

"I won't allow you to leave. You mean too much to me. I mean too much to you."

"Don't delude yourself. It's not your choice. It's mine to make and I have decided this pleasure is pretty poison. The only logical consequence of your need for total control is destruction. And, that maybe fine for you, but it's not my goal. So, before I do something stupid like let the world know that you forced yourself upon me and paid me with church funds, I will leave and we can go back to our lives as they were before we…"

"I won't let you leave me. I won't let you shame me this way. Toss me aside as if I were a broken toy."

Pitiful naked Amos is shouting from the doorway to the kitchen. He is initiating a temper tantrum. The pitch of his voice is tenor…almost soprano. His skin is flushed. His fists are clenched. His eyes begin to tear. Sarah is detached, cool and calculating. She felt this day coming for sometime and she is properly prepared to deal with his infantilism. Ignore it. She is quietly straightening the office mess. She has decided what must happen. And that is that. He turns into the kitchen only to spin around and return.

"If you are set on leaving me, so be it. I know I can't stop you. But, please, can we do it one last time for good memories?"

"As your harlot, I will charge you an extra $50. Let's go to the living room couch. I'll treat you to something special. Stretch out on the couch."

Sarah begins coaxing him.

"Mrs. Dracal, I appreciate you bringing me back to the library. When we accidentally came across it before, Jimmy and I thought it was a very interesting room. Maybe I should get Jimmy? I'm sure he'd like to hear more about the library."

"Don't bother, you can tell him whatever you want later. The room is styled after a Keep. Do you know what a Keep is?"

"Yes, a safe place in a castle."

"Dr. Dracal had all manner of wood and stone imported from his homeland to build his library. Those elements are in the walls, the floor, and the furniture."

Michael doesn't see the gargoyles over the entrance, and Mrs. Dracal has to unlock the door.

"These books contain wisdom from the ages, handed down from generations that started before your Jesus. There are words and ideas in these books that very few people have heard or would understand if they heard them. I understand only a small portion of the material. My husband understands much. Gene was learning. When he learned enough, he was to become the leader... the earthly father. Now he is gone. There is no one to use the power. The knowledge in these books can produce great power. Power over people. Power through the ages. And that power was to belong to Gene, and...."

As she extols the importance of the books and the information in them, Mrs. Dracal's eyes run from Michael's head to waist like scanners. Looking for something. She takes his hand so he can feel the ornate hand-carved edges on the desk. Her touch is cold and clammy, yet the room is warm and dry.

"Have you ever thought of learning more than any other man?"

"No ma'am."

"Michael, don't be small. The opportunity for immortal greatness is in this room. Dr. Dracal and I were thinking that you might be interested in learning the secrets of the ancients. We thought you would be interested in all the power of thousands of years. Interested in becoming the leader...the father. Just as it was to be for Gene, it can be for you."

Angelica has removed the facial shroud and now holds both Michael's hands firmly. She stares into his eyes and moves to within inches of him. He can feel her cold breath on his face and neck. She drops his hands and clasps his cheeks. Eyes are locked onto each other. She is sniffing like an animal in search of a prize. Short staccato-like nasal inhalations and exhalations course his face, neck and head. His skin chills.

"Ma'am, please. This is very uncomfortable. You're Gene's mother."

"Gene was not my son. He was born of another, years before Dr. Dracal and I met. I have no children...yet. I am, as they say, empty. Dr. Dracal is not able to give me children, but he insists that I should have them. He insists that I can choose anyone in the world. Tell me, are you pure?"

Her nose touches his. She tilts her head and brushes her lips on his. Part of Michael responds as she knew it would. She bites his lower lip. He pushes her away before her tongue can explore his mouth. With a sly grin she runs her tongue over her front teeth where she had drawn his blood.

"That hurt. Mrs. Dracal, this is crazy and very wrong. I don't know what else to say. What you are doing is just not right. What you're talking about makes no sense to me. And, I don't know what you mean by pure."

His protests fall on deaf ears. Angelica is already gliding her hands over him. Again searching. He thrashes to extricate himself from this bizarre situation.

"Michael, are you in the library? Come on, I've got to get Mary Ruth home. Are you coming or staying?"

"I'm ready to leave."

His eyes flash anger at the seductress. She smacks her lips and smiles at him.

"You are pure."

The carving knife pierces the back of Sarah's neck on the first pass. Instantly, her jaw clamps closed and her mouth is filled with Amos' former member. Blood from the wounds in both bodies splatters on the couch and rug. She rises to run. Amos cuts across her breasts as both fornicators scream.

"Bitch. Whore of Babylon. Pernicious harlot. If you don't want me, no one will want you. Ever."

She spits out his flesh.

"As a man you are a failure. Without your little game of rape the secretary, you can't even get hard. Are you a faggot?"

Sarah reaches the lamp on the table and plunges it into Amos. The glass base and three bulbs explode, shredding his face and upper torso. Blindly, he lashes out and lops off her left ear. They roll onto the floor. Grappling, not for life, but for superiority. Her hands are on his right wrist to prevent further attacks. He pulls her hair with his left and slams her head against the corner of the table. The hard wood point goes two inches into her forehead. Sara goes limp. Amos plunges the knife into her stomach and pushes it upward toward her throat. Guts flop out of the corpse and ooze down toward her feet. He rises triumphant above her, pauses for a moment and thrusts the knife into his throat. Their bodily fluids mingle for the last time. The carnage is complete.

Sarah's parents call the police, who discover the bloodbath. On the wall of the living room written in blood are the words: ***Er Ist***. The police, Sarah's parents, and the elders of the congregation agree the murder-suicide must be portrayed as a home invasion with a double murder. The letters, **E.R.I.S.T.**, on the wall are some gang code. The community is well warned and sufficiently frightened that guard dog and handgun sales increase in the next ten days. The police place all the information in a locked file. Sometimes it's better to not tell the truth.

POLICE

"Michael. Michael, are you in the barn?"

"Yes, Mother. What do you want?"

"Deputy Gingrich is here and he wants to talk to you."

In two minutes, the overweight, middle-aged former school janitor is standing in the barn doorway. His girth, augmented by the belt with all the necessary utilities, causes him to seem larger than reality. A purposeful attempt at intimidation. The deputy is the prototype bully. He attempts to push around the teens and he fawns at their parents. Michael has nothing to fear from the deputy; besides Aaron is up in the loft.

"Mikey, I understand that you were at Gene Dracal's the night he died."

"Yes sir."

"I have it on good authority that you and Jimmy Hauck went there with guns to threaten Gene and his friends."

"No sir, that's not true."

"I further understand that you and Jimmy beat up Gene and then left."

"That's not true either, sir."

"If what I have said is not true, why don't you tell me your version of the truth?"

"Before I say anything, I want to know why you are questioning me."

"We're just trying to get all the details of that night from everybody that was involved. And you were there, so you're involved. Now, tell me what you know."

"Maybe I should see if my father and grandfather would like to be here while you question me."

"I am not questioning you like you were a suspect. I'm asking for your point-of-view as to the facts of that night. And, I certainly don't need to talk to them. I need you to tell me what happened the night Gene Dracal died. Why you went there? What you did there?"

"Before I get in trouble or say something, which may not be true, I think I need to have my dad here."

"If you and your dad would like to come to the station that would be fine. I was hoping, for your sake, we could keep your father out of this. I was hoping we wouldn't have to make this formal with all the forms and records. If you just tell me what I want to know, I'll be on my way. And no one has to know I was here, or what I asked. Or, maybe we should all go to the office and make this an official event."

"Are you arresting me?"

"No, but if I have to arrest you to get answers to my questions, I will. What's the harm in you telling me your side of what happened that night?"

"Nothing I guess."

"Well…"

Michael relates as much of the night as he can remember. His story stops when they all go to Mary Ruth's for his treatment.

"So, you're saying you didn't know Jimmy had a gun with him when you got out of the truck?"

"Yes sir."

"And, that he saved you from a beating."

"Yes sir. Ask Mary Ruth. She stayed with Jimmy in the truck."

"I already spoke to her. She told me her version of why you three were there. And she claims she fell asleep while you were at the pool with Gene. Jimmy woke her when he returned to the truck with you draped over his shoulders."

"So you see, I'm not lying. Why all the fuss over my visit?"

"Funny thing about the accident that killed the boys. There were no skid marks up to the crash. It looks like there were no brakes applied. When we went over the wreckage, we discovered that the brake lines were dry. There was no fluid, so the brakes wouldn't work if they were applied. It also seems that the lines were opened, the fluid bled, and the lines reconnected. So we went back to the Dracals and discovered a large spill of brake fluid in the driveway. It's more than strange, we think it's murder. Mary Ruth was obviously not involved. I don't think she would know a brake line from a clothesline. And, she corroborates your story. See, that was easy. The truth always is. That leaves Jimmy. He's next on my list. Do you know where he is?"

"No sir, I don't."

"It doesn't matter; I'll find him. Thanks for your cooperation. And we'll just leave it that you and I had a nice private conversation. No one has to know."

With that, the deputy turns and wobbles back to his car. The lump in Michael's stomach feels bigger than a basketball. Murder. He hears Aaron climbing down the ladder.

"What did Deputy Gingrich want, Michael?"

"He was just asking if I knew anything about the accident the other night. I told him no. He said he was asking all of Gene's classmates and friends. I was just one on a list."

The day drags on until Jimmy arrives in a cloud of dust.

"What the hell did you tell Deputy Gingrich?"

"You mean about the night of Gene's party?"

"Yeah, about that night."

"I told him the truth. How I went to see Gene, and why. How you and Mary Ruth stayed in the truck. How you came to my rescue. How you must have fired the rifle, and carried me back to the truck"

"Are you sure that's all you told him?"

"Yes, I'm sure. Why?"

"He just about accused me of murder. He said the brakes were bled so that they wouldn't work. He said that I had time, means, and motive to do this. I was a suspect. But, here is the weird thing. He said that Mary Ruth said that she fell asleep in the truck, while you were with Gene. I can't verify that or nothing 'cause I fell asleep. I fell asleep 'cause I had drunk a few beers that night before Mary Ruth showed up at my door with her clothes all torn. So sittin' in the truck, I dozed off. Then she screams me awake. She hears the commotion from the pool and says you're probably in real trouble. She hollers that I should get my rifle from the lock box in the back of the truck and go to the pool and save you. I must have been in a deep sleep, 'cause I fumbled with the lock and the rifle. Then Mary Ruth and I went around the house and saved you. I'm in deep trouble, but I did nothin' wrong. In fact, I did something good. I saved you. Now you gotta save me. Deputy Gingrich said that I needed to bring my truck down to the sheriff's office today. They need to examine it. What am I gonna do?"

"You're gonna take the truck to the office like they asked. Take your dad. He'll know what to do? Gingrich doesn't like to be tough to kids when their parents are around. I'm sorry; I can't do more than that to help."

Why would Jimmy want to hurt the boys? Maybe he just wanted to disable the car so they wouldn't follow us. It's sad how he went too far. How his actions got out of control for no other reason than he just didn't think.

"Aaron. Did you hear all that? What do you make of it?

"I make that Jimmy is in serious trouble. He did something real dumb that got a bunch of kids killed. It would take a real expensive lawyer to keep him from going to jail forever. And, Mr. Hauck spent all his money on Jimmy's brother. He only got eight years for killin' that guy at the bar. Should have got life or the chair. Those Hauck brothers are real angry. Now, Jimmy is gonna pay for both crimes, 'cause the money's gone."

"I'm confused. I thought Jimmy wouldn't do such a thing. Destruction of property is bad enough. But, murder. Why would he do it?"

"We'll probably never know. Just like we'll never know what really happened to Sarah and the pastor."

The boys are absolutely still and stare at each other. Michael senses that Aaron wants to unburden his soul, but he can't initiate the conversation. He sees tears well in Aaron's eyes and his body tremble slightly.

"It drives me crazy to think what she must have been going through as the thugs killed her. The police said she died of multiple stab wounds to her neck and body. What would drive punks to such frenzy that they attack the two of them for no reason? I mean, they're sitting at the desk doing church work. They hear a knock at the door. Pastor Zug gets up to answer it and is stabbed in the doorway. Sarah had no warning. She couldn't run or hide. The thugs rush in and slash her to death. Then they rob what little there is in the house and run like rats. Where's the sense to all that? Michael, what with Jimmy and the murdering thugs, it seems to me that the sense is going out of the world."

"Maybe you're right."

Michael puts his arm around his brother's shoulders and they walk to the house for dinner. The bond is eternal.

After clearing the table, Michael looks for Neen. He went back to his house. The boy follows. He notices a small coupe parked beneath the elm tree beside the house. The lights are on and two forms are seated by the table in the kitchen.

"Grandfather, it's me can I come in?"

"Sure. You're always welcome."

Reading the bible and writing notes on a legal pad is Vincent. He turns pages and goes back then forward, then back again.

"Good evening, Michael. How are you?"

"OK."

"Just OK?"

"It's nothin'. What are you two working on?"

"Michael, your father demanded that you not be involved in our activities as they pertain to the stones and the Tal. I have to honor my son's wishes."

"Grandfather, you always told me that I should stand up for my beliefs. I should do what I think is right, regardless of criticism from others. It's the way you have lived. It's the way Father has lived. So, it's the way I will live. I am man enough to take the consequences of my actions. I'm man enough to stand up to Father, when I am convinced he is wrong. That's the way you are. And I know he would stand up to his father, if he felt his father was wrong. I come from a long line of stubborn Dutchmen. So I want you to tell me what you're doing."

"Your grandfather gave me the family bible to read. Specifically, I was interested in the history on the back pages. I have learned much and the names and dates have raised many questions. I am still searching for answers. Here, let me show you something. Do you see this page that was removed from the bible? My first question is why was it removed; yet not thrown away? After I examined the book, I noticed other pages had been removed. They are missing, but this one was saved. Why? One answer could be that those who were creating the history decided to re-write it by eliminating parts of it. They may have decided to recount their version of history rather than the objective truth. Maybe they were ashamed or frightened by what happened. A certain ancestor named Mihai is noted to have killed and been killed by these four: Genber, Chzrut, Trelech, and Nooem. Obviously there was a significant conflict. The names of all five are ancient. We don't see them today or even two hundred years ago. The four men, other than Mihai, were, most likely, considered evil. Or they had done something evil. Obviously, they were outsiders. Perhaps they were interlopers from a valley nearby. The name Mihai is an ancient way of spelling of Michael. Or, better said, Michael is a modern version of Mihai. Now, we saw the names of the all five men on the plaque in the building in the Tal; those who were killed by your ancestor were in a star and the name Mihai was upside down on the bottom of plaque. We can assume the four were somehow connected to the building and they were favored, while Mihai was the intruder. Having seen the architecture of the building, I am sure it was some form of ancient religious setting. Why else would there be an altar? Therefore, we assume the four worshipped there."

"If the men worshipped at the Tal and were killed by my ancestor, it could have been some form of conflict based on religion. My studies at the college report that the religious sects and factions that came to this country, Pilgrims, Quakers, Mennonites, and the like were very strict and held tightly the laws of their faiths. It's what held the small sects together when they were escaping Europe in small boats. And, it's what kept the sects together when they struggled for a new life against the Indians, the environment, and the elements. The Europeans called this period of history the *Holy Experiment*. And with every experiment there is trial and error, or mistake and progress. These religious zealots believed conflict and absorption overcame errors and mistakes. By taking command. By ruling the defeated."

"I told you he was smart, professor. He's smarter than his dad and me put together. He takes classes at the college. Michael, if it were a religious war, what do you think they were fighting over?"

"To them, any war was a religious war, because they believed God was their leader, who had temporal commanders. These people fought the Indians over farmland and water. And always did it in the name of their God. They felt they were required to crush the heathen. It was God's command. They were in constant conflict with other sects for land and souls. They fought each other's sects, like warring nations. They wanted to conquer and obliterate all heathen, white or brown. And anyone who did not believe as they did was heathen. Maybe they equated the size of their following to fulfilling God's will. God sent them to this land to build a better world. The larger the sect, the better the sect's chance of survival in a hostile environment. And they wanted to survive to reap the joy of this Promised Land. So they went to war to increase their flocks. It was their divine right to kill and conquer."

"This speculation is very interesting. There are many more questions, which need to be addressed. Questions that can't be answered in a college classroom or found in a textbook. That's why your grandfather and I are going back to the Tal tonight. We can't ask you to go, because that would violate your father's trust. It would put you in danger with him. However, there may well be a time very soon when you will need to go back to the Tal with us. When that time is upon us, we will have to talk to your father. Just not tonight."

Although Michael was pleased to be part of this adventure again, he was not disappointed that he would not be going with the men tonight. With all he had been through in the last few days, including the visit from the Deputy, Michael wanted a nice dinner and to go to bed early. Tomorrow he can learn what the two men found in the Tal. The kitchen smelled like roast chicken.

"Michael, Mrs. Dracal called while you were with your grandfather. She has some things of Gene's that she thought you'd like to have. Some school things. She wondered if you could go to her house tonight and look at the items. She stressed tonight, because she and the Doctor are leaving tomorrow and won't be back. I told her you didn't drive yet, but Aaron could take you over to her house."

"Eat up, baby brother, your taxi is ready."

Dread coats Michael like heavy oil. He has to sustain the charade. Mother must never know. His hand is clammy on the truck's door handle.

"Maybe Gene's ol' lady will give you his black book. I have heard he was a real stud. You could use all the help you can get in that area, I'm sure. It's kinda creepy goin' through a dead guy's stuff and figurin' out what you want, and who got the good stuff before you arrived. Do you think Gene's ol' lady would mind if I took some stuff, if I thought it was neat? I could tell her it would be a testimony to his memory. How's that?"

"This whole thing is too weird for words. Can you keep a secret?"

"Sure, if I have to."

"You have to."

Michael provides a cursory outline of his chance meeting with Mrs. Dracal in the library, and how she fell upon him. How he was saved by Jimmy's need to take Mary Ruth home.

96

"She kissed you. Dang. My baby brother has an older sweetie. You'll be OK. I'm here to protect you. If she grabs you again, I'll save you. I'll step between you two and let her grab me anywhere she wants."

The pickup crunches over the driveway and stops at the front door. There are no outside lights and very few lights inside. Aaron knocks. Mrs. Dracal answers.

"Michael, thank you for coming on such short notice. I'm sorry if doing me this favor inconveniences you. You must be Aaron. Welcome to our house. Thank you for taking the time to bring Michael here."

Inside, the boys notice that sheets cover all the furniture and there is no art on the walls. No doubt about it. The Dracals are going away for a long time.

"As you can see, we are closing the house. The staff has been instructed to get everything ready for storage. The house will be put up for sale within a few weeks. There is no reason for us to stay here any longer. Aaron, would you like something to drink or some cookies? We're cleaning out the pantry and the kitchen. The housekeeper will throw away anything not eaten before we leave. You're welcome to anything you find. I believe there are few beers in the refrigerator. Help yourself. I need to discuss Gene's belongings with Michael. It won't take long. You can wait for him in the kitchen."

Aaron walks through the dining room and into the kitchen.

The two men very cautiously approach the ninth section of the fence, pry apart the boards for an entrance, and slip over the crest of the hill into the Tal. Each has a damp cross on his forehead, and carries a powerful flashlight, numerous plastic food bags and plastic jars, and a long rope in his backpack. They are on a special spelunking adventure. The pace quickens as they descend toward the building. Heartbeats quicken, too.

"What are we looking for?"

"I hope we can learn more about the building, specifically the altar and the tunnel beneath it. Tonight, I'm going to lower you deeper than you and Michael went before. I need to confirm my suspicions of the shaft. I think it's a passageway. This time you're going to take samples of the earth. But, we have to hurry. I don't want to be in the Tal or the building when the lightning starts."

The nearer they get to the Keep, the more pronounced is the odor. In the darkness, Neen sees movement, like an animal darting from the fortress to the woods.

"*Vincent, did you see the wolf?*"

"*I saw something. I'm not sure what it was. Just keep going. We're safe for now.*"

"*There's another running around the corner of the building.*"

"*I saw it.*"

"*It can't be a wolf, it has no tail. But, it runs like a wolf…on all fours and kind of slinky.*"

"*Not quite like a wolf. It doesn't run front-back. It runs right-left like a human.*"

"*Wolves run right-left, too.*"

"*Only when they're trotting or loping, not when they're sprinting. And that thing was sprinting.*"

"*What are those noises from the bushes?*"

"*More of the moving shadows. As I said, I think we're safe for now. But, we can't just take our time; speed is critical. Tell me what you note about the building.*"

"*It's facing north-south. All churches that I've ever seen face east-west to greet the rising sun. The building seems to sit on a berm, like it was intentionally raised. There are no steps leading into the building. Just a slope. No windows, of course. No steeple. A domed roof, not a pointed one. More like a mosque than a church.*"

"*Inside many churches, the ceiling looks like a boat inverted. That's why they have pointed roofs. This is a different exterior shape, like a coliseum turned upside down.*"

"*The double door is in good shape, for a building, which is probably hundreds of years old. That's strange.*"

"*And there is only a little oxidation on the metal hinges and handles.*"

"*Like the doorway is active and well tended. Make sure you note all this. We will need to compare our notes later.*"

"*When we were here the last time, I thought there was something special about the floor and walls inside. Now I can see. The floor is one continuous slab. It couldn't be concrete, so it has to be solid rock. And the walls are the same rock, like this building was carved out of a huge rock protrusion.*"

"I've gathered the material I want you to see in the library."

Michael follows Angelica Dracal down the narrow hall to the windowless room. Candles illuminate the entrance. Dr. Dracal is at the desk. He barely acknowledges Michael's presence, except with numerous short and shallow breaths.

"Thank you for coming here tonight. Angelica has told me that she only had a brief moment to discuss the opportunity we are offering you. I would like to provide you more details, so you may have a better grasp of the magnitude of your opportunity."

Michael does not hear the door close. The candle flames do not flicker a warning.

"In this room is a collection of wisdom that transcends your understanding of time and space. Wisdom that can make its possessor the greatest ruler of all ages. The ruler, not just of a country or a continent, but the ruler of the world. Can you comprehend the scope of what is before you?"

"No sir."

"This is not something for anyone or everyone. This earthly power can be bestowed upon only one. One, chosen above all others. And the choice is ours to make because we have been empowered by the one true god to make it. Yahweh, the avenger of the downtrodden, the righter of wrongs, greater than all others, has given us the power to choose someone to rule the earth. Although I have vast knowledge, I can not be the leader. The leader must learn and be versed in the ways of Yahweh. I have done that. And the leader must be pure to produce offspring with Yahweh's handmaiden. I cannot fulfill this second task. I am the counselor. The guide into this world of power and might. Angelica was chosen by Yahweh to be the vessel of procreation. She is his handmaiden. She is fertile. We had thought it was to be Gene, with whom she should lie. We taught him much. He was a willing student. But, he defiled himself and became impure, before he could lie with Angelica. His impurity culminated in his death. We were obviously wrong to trust Gene. But, he was a sign. A symbol of who was to be the leader. We now know the leader is to be you. It is you who are to be taught. It is you who must be with Angelica and produce offspring for Yahweh. Do you understand what I am saying?"

"No sir. As I told your wife, it makes no sense to me whatsoever. I'm upset that you lied to my mother and me. You tricked me into being here tonight. I guess I should have expected it, but I didn't. I am not yet sixteen. There is much I have to learn, but what you are proposing I learn does not interest me. In fact, it frightens me. You frighten me. Third, I understand what you are suggesting about me and Mrs. Dracal. She's your wife. Because you don't think of her that way is your problem and I don't want to be part of your problem. Your problem frightens me most of all. I mean no disrespect, ma'am, but I'm not ready to do what you're suggesting. I'm going to leave now. And, I promise I won't speak of this night to anyone when you're gone."

"Well, we had hoped you would see the glory of our offer. Let me explain it to you in better, more convincing terms. If you don't do what we offer, we have the power and authority to change your mind. It is better that you willingly act as we wish, but we will do anything to get our way. We can inflict anguish so severe that you will seek relief from it. The relief that you receive will be to do what we are offering now. This relief will let you rise above your boring everyday existence. And you'll see that ours was the right path to choose. If you leave now, know that we will meet again under much different circumstances. Then you will do as we summon."

"Look at the altar and the plank at its base, the one we moved. I drew a cross on each. The crosses have turned black and almost burned into the stone and wood. Help me move the altar far to the side, so we can move two planks and create a large opening. We have enough rope for you to go about fifty feet down. You'll need the bags, jars, and this knife."

The knife handed Isaac is rusted and looks as if it were forged centuries ago. The dirk's handle is wrapped in cloth, which has been tied with leather strips. The cloth has been moistened. As Vincent wraps the rope three times around the altar, Isaac weaves his end between his legs and around his waist...double wrapped for safety and comfort.

"We'll do this in ten-foot stops. Cut into the walls and place what you can into the bags or jars. We don't need huge chunks. Keep separate what you get at each stop. And, talk to me. Tell me everything you experience. Shape, color, and texture. Ready?"

"Ready."

Isaac slides into the maw.

"First stop."

"This appears to be a shaft cut out of the stone slab. That means the slab upon which the building sits may be as big as a mountain. Small clumps of earth are stuck to the walls. Nothing spectacular. Nothing moving. No real color except for gray. The stench is pervasive. OK let's go."

"Second stop."

"As you were lowering me, I thought I saw something moving. Like the last

time I was here. About the size of one of those house cats that goes wild and puts on twenty-five pounds. I can't figure out where it came from or went or how it held on to the wall of the shaft. I think I saw an opening in the wall, but it was a shadow created by a small outcrop. The smell is getting worse. And, it's definitely getting warmer. It should be getting cooler as I go deeper into the earth. I am scraping bits of the wall and the earth clods for your collection. Nothing spectacular."

"Third stop. You are getting heavy. I can barely see your light."

"Just more of the same down here, only more so. More outcrops that look like they could be exits from the shaft. Two more things moved. My reflexes are just not fast enough to catch a clear look. I hear it and by the time I respond it's gone. The rock on the walls seems to be getting darker. Maybe it's my eyes getting accustomed to the pitch black. The flashlight doesn't reflect off the walls as much down here as it did above. I think I see an occasional lighter stone with some color. I have retrieved two of these. Michael would like these for his collection."

"Fourth stop. The weight is beginning to strain me and the altar."

"The walls are definitely darker. The stone looks almost charred. Charred stone is strange. That can only be the result of incredible heat. Heat like nothing else on earth. I can break off small bits easily. I haven't seen any movement on the walls. Maybe I frightened them away. I have seen a few very small fissures. Barely wide enough to insert the knife's point. Now it's cold. First it was warm, then hot. Now cold. That's not normal. When we come back, I'll bring a jacket. The smell is deeper. More of a sulfur content and less rotting protein. Bad gas, not dead flesh. I think I can hear what sounds like rushing wind. It can't be wind, because I don't feel a breeze. It could be water. Or the flutter of thousands of bird wings. Maybe bats. This place would be perfect for bats."

The weight of the man at the end of the rope tugs the altar. He hears and feels the sliding of the large stone. Vincent fears it will tumble in.

"Fifth and last stop. Just look around and I'll pull you up immediately."

"It's got to be water. It sounds like it's a hundred yards away, maybe farther. Maybe a quarter of a mile. Maybe a half mile. I wonder if that's what makes the air so danged cold. Wait. It just got real hot. First I can see my breath. Now I can barely catch it for the heat. It must be well over a hundred. The air currents are extremes of cold and heat. My fingers are beginning to get numb, but I'm sweating like on an August noon. The black walls seem to be littered with jagged pieces of stone. I have this feeling I've seen these colors before. My eyes must be tricking me. I don't mean to be crude, but the odor is worse than before. Like when one of the

Guernseys has to be cleaned out. The bags and jars are filled. If you're ready, I'm ready. This is scaring me."

It takes all of Vincent's strength to extract the older man. Isaac sits and catches his breath. Vincent coils the rope and checks his watch.

"It's a little past time for us to leave. I'll take the ropes if you carry the specimens. Let's put back the plank and altar. Hurry".

Isaac sees the planks and the altar anointed, this time in several places. Vincent anoints the floor of the Keep, the door, and the doorway. The two trudge back up the hill. Behind them hundreds of eyes glare. Small shapes and forms scurry around the Keep… inside and out. Thunder reverberates in the night sky. A huge flash illuminates the two as they head back up the hill toward the farm. The first strike hits the Tal as Isaac replaces the fence boards. He thinks he hears shrieks from over the hill. They walk right past something hiding in the weeds. The crash of thunder masks the form's short shallow panting.

REBECCA

The crash of pots and pans reverberates throughout the house and into the barn. Before anyone can react, the hysterical screams of Twyla Glee pierce the post-crash silence.

"Daddy, Michael, Aaron, come here quick. Something terrible is happening."

Three strong torsos and six strong legs race for the back door. On the kitchen floor among the cooking ware is Rebecca, ashen and bloody. Kneeling over her, Twyla Glee has no idea what to do except sob.

"What happened?"

"I don't know. We were getting dinner ready and all of a sudden Mommy collapsed. There's blood everywhere. Look!"

"Twyla Glee, try to relax. Boys, go to the laundry and get as many clean towels as you can find. Then get ice from the freezer and make ice bags with a few towels. Now. Twyla Glee, get down on the floor next to you mother. Hold her hand and talk to her."

Ruben surveys the situation. Blood is oozing from Rebecca's nose and her saliva is pink. The outpouring has discolored her blouse and waist of her skirt. She is so pale, yet she is burning to the touch. With a fever this intense, she should be flush. He looks at his daughter and notices the first drop of blood below her right nostril. His touch of her forehead finds warmth.

"Apply the ice bags to you mother's nose, forehead, and the back of her neck. Becky, can you hear me?"

Her eyelids flutter. He sees the blank stare of someone in serious trouble.

"Becky, we're going to get you to the hospital. They will be able to stanch the blood and attack the fever. Do you understand?"

She gives a perceptible nod. Her lips purse to send a kiss.

"Boys, make sure your sister gets ice packs just like your mother. We're going to take them both to the hospital. Michael, call Dr. Hoffman, tell him what is happening and ask him to meet us at County General. Aaron, get the 350 and pile the bed with blankets and quilts… all you can find. Take them off the beds, as well as out of the closets and cedar chest. We'll use the truck bed as a mobile stretcher. I'll stay here. Do you know where your grandfather is?"

"I think he went to visit Vincent at the Dutchland."

"After you call Dr. Hoffman, call the motel and tell your grandfather what's going on."

"Daddy, what's happening to Momma and me?"

"I don't know sweetheart, but the doctors at the hospital will be able to fix this right up. So, don't worry. Be brave, and know that your family is here with you."

Ruben looks at the towel on his wife's face. It is drenched in the red essence of her life. Quickly he removes the towel, rewraps the ice pack in a clean towel, and reapplies it.

"Daddy, I'm bleeding all over my blouse. I can't stop the bleeding."

"Lie on the floor and keep the cold compress on your nose, honey. It will only be a few minutes before we can get you to the hospital. Here, use a fresh towel."

"Daddy, there's blood in my mouth."

He panics. If blood is oozing from his wife's mouth, it may be going down her throat; she could choke on the clots. So could Twyla Glee.

"Put a rolled up towel under your head and spit out the blood in your mouth. Don't swallow it."

He lifts Becky into a sitting position and her head bobs to her chest. The second compress is blood soaked. He props up her head and applies a third towel to her nose. Then he tilts her head forward to slow the ingestion of blood.

"Becky, if you can hear me, I want you to spit or just open your mouth and let the blood pour out. I don't want you to swallow it."

She doesn't open her eyes but nods. The floor around them is slippery.

"Father, I reached Dr. Hoffman's office and told them. I reached Neen at the motel. He'll meet us at the hospital."

"I got the truck bed loaded with blankets. I backed the truck up to the backdoor. We're ready."

"Aaron, pick up your sister and carry her to the truck. Michael, hold open the door and then get on to truck bed to help load the women. Grab the clean towels."

The forty-step journey cannot be hurried lest the women bounce or hit something, yet the bearers cannot tarry, lest treatment be delayed. Michael slides the women to the front of the bed so that their backs are propped in a seated position. Ruben sits next to his wife and applies the ice packs. Michael is responsible for Twyla Glee. Aaron exceeds the speed limit with his lights on and horn honking. The tires' screech punctuates the truck's arrival at the ER entrance to the hospital. Gurneys accompanied by nurses are loaded and the women are taken through double doors for examination.

"Park the truck and join us."

"Mr. Hess, can you tell us what happened?"

The details, as much as he knows, are parsed out. Doctors and nurses poke, prod, and listen. Breathing masks are applied and blood drawn. Ruben has no comprehension of the terms and codes used by these angels of mercy.

"Sir, as of now, we have no idea what is causing the bleeding. We believe we have slowed it somewhat. Until we determine the cause of the affliction, we are unable to treat it properly. We will continue to infuse new blood so that there is no damage caused by the extensive loss of this fluid. We will continue to facilitate breathing and stabilize the fever in both women. Dr. Hoffman will be here shortly. We will confer with him and he will advise you of the course of action he deems appropriate."

"Here he is now."

"Ruben. Michael. Give me a few minutes to talk to the attending physician and then I will come to the waiting room."

"Sit here, son. Your brother and grandfather will be along."

"Ruben, what happened?"

The events are retold.

"I think we should pray."

The four men kneel and hold hands, while Isaac intones in the language of the bible. Certain words and phrases sound familiar.

"Most high... most beloved... protector of your children... defender of those who love you... fight against pestilence... heal the infirmed..."

Their amen is echoed by Dr. Hoffman in the doorway. He pulls the men aside and speaks calmly.

"There is much we don't know, but there are some things we do. First, Rebecca and Twyla Glee appear to be suffering from a form of virus. That could explain the combination of the high fever and profuse bleeding. In general terms, this virus is referred to as hemorrhagic fever, which causes profuse discharge from the vessels. There are many and diverse forms of hemorrhagic fever. Some are quite common and are related to HIV and AIDS, and some are rare and occur mostly in isolated parts of Africa. Outbreaks of these forms are caused by illnesses carried by monkeys and other animals. The monkeys are immune to the disease. They act as hosts. This disease is devastatingly deadly, and has been known to wipe out entire villages and tribes. Since, neither Rebecca nor Twyla Glee has come into contact with anyone afflicted with AIDS nor has either received a transfusion in the past ten years, we can safely rule out that area. Further, since they have had no contact with monkeys or other infected animals that we know of, we can eliminate that area. While this narrows our field of examination, it still leaves the basic question unanswered: What exactly has afflicted them? Once we know this, proper treatment can be addressed. Therefore, I am going to send samples of their blood to the Centers for Disease Control in Atlanta for a thorough analysis. I alerted an old friend of mine at the CDC, that I was sending blood samples for his personal review and analysis. I will also need to send samples of your blood and that of your sons to the CDC. Since you came in contact with the blood of the women, it is possible that you have been infected. We will take the five samples to the airport. He will get the samples by 9 tonight. He told me that his analysis would take 36-48 hours. We're going to scan a smear of each blood sample into the hospital's computer and e-mail that to Dr. Lehman. We can view the same smear and confer on the telephone how to provide relief, until he has completed his analysis. Right now, the women are resting as comfortably as possible. We have applied chemical compresses to the external bleeding. We have tubes to withdraw any blood that may get to the stomach. Breathing assistance is in place. And, we are attempting to transfuse new blood to replace the tainted blood in them. These are temporary measures, until we know what specific course of action is appropriate. One last item: I want you three to shower and change into hospital scrubs immediately. When you leave this room, I'll have it disinfected and quarantined. This way we can contain the illness. Now, what questions can I answer?"

"When can we come back and see Becky and my daughter?"

"In about a half an hour, after you're clean. Give us the time to check all the support systems and make sure they are working properly."

"Will Rebecca and Twyla Glee be all right?"

"I believe so, but there is always danger in the treatment of uncontrolled bleeding. Certain medications can clot the blood and stop the bleeding, but these clots can produce problematic side effects. We must determine the cause so we can use the right medicine. Numerous sera and antitoxins are available, so I'm confident we can treat the issue. Along these lines when you visit with the women, it would be helpful if you can determine what they were doing or did twenty-four hours prior to the onset of the disease. They may not be responsive at first, but you have to keep trying. It's imperative that we know all that went on before they collapsed. It is probably something they did together. I hope neither one gave the disease to the other."

"I can tell you this now. Yesterday, Becky and I spent a good portion of the afternoon at the kitchen table goin' over bills and expenses and an upcoming event. Nothing out of the ordinary yesterday or last night for her. In the morning I went to check the chickens in the coops. It's their time to start to lay. Got to separate the layers from the pullets and get the roosters in a different pen. Not sure what Becky did this morning."

"Twyla Glee did laundry chores yesterday. Aaron and me did the bedrooms and bathrooms and she did laundry and helped mother in the kitchen. They were makin' food for the next few days, and puttin' it in the refrigerator or freezer. I think she said they were going to take some to Neen's house for those times he likes to eat alone. I think they did that this morning."

"That's a good start. If you can get any more details from them, particularly about this morning, it could be helpful. I stress this morning, because this type of fever has a rapid onset. Little incubation time."

"I've got to get on the computer with Dr. Lehman. Let me call you or you call me when either of us have more information."

Four somber faces enter the double room. On the two beds, attached to all manner of life support and monitoring systems, lay their loved ones. The four brave and true are helpless. They can only observe.

"You can sit by the side of the bed and talk through the plastic cover. But don't lift the cover for any reason."

The nurse in attendance quietly exits. This is family time. The whoosh of the air being pumped into and out of the plastic tent that covers each woman augments the beeps and pings. The combination of sounds creates syncopation, which would be almost humorous except for the circumstance.

"Becky, in case you don't know it, you're in County General hospital. And we're all here with you. Aaron, Michael, Isaac, and I will be by your side until you can walk out of the hospital. Dr. Hoffman is in control of the situation and he tells me you're doing just fine. Can you hear me?"

No response.

"Move your right hand if you can hear me."

The twitch to the right and left is more welcome than a blazing fireplace on a snowy day.

"Move your left hand if you think you can answer questions."

No response.

"That's all right my love. I can do all the talking for both of us. I'm not going away, I am moving over to Twyla Glee's bed."

"Sweetheart, it's Daddy. How do you feel?"

Pale dry lips whisper *tired… and hot.*

"Your brothers, grandfather and I are here. We'll stay until you get well. Can you open your eyes?"

Fine slits appear on either side of her nose. She struggles to focus and see through the plastic cover. Her smile is feint but visible.

"Sweetheart, do you feel strong enough to answer a few questions?"

Her eyes are open now and she seems to comprehend her surroundings. She nods.

"I'll ask you questions which can be answered yes or no. When your answer is yes, raise your right hand up and down. When the answer is no wave your right hand left and right. Is that clear?"

Her right hand goes up and down.

"I understand you and your mother cooked this morning. Did you cook anything different or special?"

Left and right.

"Did you and your mother take any food in those plastic containers to your grandfather's house?"

Up and down.

"Did you put the containers in his refrigerator?"

Up and down.

"Did you leave right after that?"

Left and right.

"Did your mother ready the house?"

Up and down.

"Did she pick up things and put them in their place?"

Up and down.

"Did you help her?"

Up and down.

"Did you touch the roots I left on the kitchen table?"

Another voice takes over. Up and down.

"Did you and your mother touch the roots?"

Up and down.

"Did you take them from the kitchen table?"

Left and right.

"Did your mother take them from the kitchen table?"

No response.

"Twyla Glee, I am not angry nor will I be angry at what you did with the roots. But, we need to know if you touched them so the doctor can treat your illness. Did your mother pick up a root and give it to you to put on the table in the living room?"

Up and down.

"That's it. We have to tell Doc Hoffman."

"Isaac, just because Becky and Twyla Glee touched some roots that were on your kitchen table, doesn't mean that this is the cause of their affliction."

"It does to me. Why don't I go to my house and retrieve a root and bring it here for the lab to analyze?"

Before anyone can argue, the old man is heading toward the door and his truck.

"Tell Doc Hoffman what we learned and tell him I'll be back with the cause of the disease in about an hour."

For these men the pieces of the puzzle are not fitting together.

"Ruben, may I talk to you alone in the hall?"

"As I told you I made slides of the five blood samples with a digital camera, which is part of an electron microscope. I e-mailed the slides to Dr. Lehman in Atlanta. Together we went over each slide as part of our initial investigation. The blood of the two women carries the same virus. The virus is not found in the blood samples of any of the three males. This means that you three did not contract the virus from the blood that you touched. Frankly that is rare. Most often this virus is passed by exposure to and ingestion of bodily fluids, such as blood, spit, or sweat. That did not happen. Dr. Lehman is relieved and confused. Relieved that the virus is isolated to the two women and confused that it is not following its predicted pattern of expansion. He concludes, and I agree, that the virus was contracted by contact with the fluids of a host foreign to Rebecca and Twyla Glee. And, you and the boys had no contact with these fluids. Therefore, you do not have the virus. He is also concerned that we must find this foreign host and eradicate it before its fluids infect others."

"Charles, Isaac thinks he knows how the women got the virus and where the host, as you call it, is now. He went to retrieve the host. He'll be back in about an hour."

"That could be very dangerous. If he touches the host, he will, like your wife and daughter, contract the virus. He shouldn't touch it. He should let me send HAZMAT people to wherever the host is. Let the professionals do what they are trained to do."

"That's the strange part. Isaac says the women got the virus from handling a root he has in his house. A root that has been in his house since the last time Becky was there. That's got to be two weeks. In that time, I'm sure he has handled the root more than once, yet your lab test shows that he does not have the virus. How can that be? How can a disease be selective in who it attacks?"

"There are too many questions to start answering them here in the hall. Let's wait until he gets back with the root."

"This is just another very bizarre event on the farm. We have been flooded with them for about three weeks."

Dr. Hoffman looks into Ruben's eyes and whispers so no one other than the two of them can hear.

"Ruben, one other thing. The blood samples under the electron microscope indicate that Rebecca is pregnant."

"Oh, God."

"It's true. I double-checked to see if it was Becky or your daughter, but it's Becky. The pregnancy is in the very preliminary stage, two weeks or less. The unfortunate thing is that with all the hemorrhaging, the zygote will simply be flushed out of her system as if she was having a severe period. She'll never know she was pregnant. I suggest you do not discuss this with her until she is fully recovered."

Ruben's eyes flash disappointment, bewilderment, and abandonment. He can't say a thing to his wife about the child they both so earnestly wanted. It was to be their special-gift child when the first three left the nest. He must sit on this knowledge and pain, and wait for the woman in his life to return to him. Maybe they can try again. The stomping of Neen's shoes shatters Ruben's interlude.

"Son, where is Dr. Hoffman?"

"I don't know. We'll have to have him paged."

In a few minutes, the three men are walking down a long sterile hall of closed brown doors, blue walls, and green floor to the lab.

"This is the root that Becky and Twyla Glee handled. This is where they got the disease."

He hands a small plastic bag to the Chief Pathologist, Dr. John Eshleman.

"We have reason to believe that the root contains some toxins or a virus which is capable of causing hemorrhagic fever. Would it be acceptable if Ruben and Isaac stayed with us while you looked at the substance? Be very careful. And, John, I'd like to send a sample of the root to Atlanta."

Dr. Eshleman nods to his colleague.

"They can stay if they stay behind me. Not beside me. Once I get a few cross sections, I'll re-bag the root, and rush it to the airport. Will Barry Lehman receive the sample?"

Dr. Hoffman nods.

Dr. Eshleman takes the unopened bag in his gloved hands and walks gingerly toward a small metal door beside a double-sized-single-pane-window facing a workstation. He places the unopened bag on a small table in the room beyond the window, closes the door, and activates the light and air systems.

He sits at the workstation and inserts his hands and arms into the gloves and sleeves, which protrude from the interior wall. With experience and respect, he opens the bag and slices off a cross section. This he places on a Petrie dish and replaces the remainder of the root in the bag. He picks up the dish and places it on a dish. Now he activates another system and a microscope slides into position. Simultaneously, a large color monitor bounces to life. The contents of the Petrie dish come into focus. With each gradual five degrees of descent, the slice is refocused and an image is taken. The fibers of the slice loom as large as oak trees. At the next stage, they disappear in closeness.

"We're as tight as we can get. Atlanta can do more, because their equipment is not twenty years old. But, I see nothing that would indicate that this is the source of the virus that infected the two women. Charlie, will you hand me the slides of the blood."

Dr. Eshleman places the color slides in the wall light box.

"That's interesting. See the straight-edged cells in the blood. These are what I believe to be the source of the disease. There are hundreds of them on each slide. My equipment restricts me from going deeper. There may be more, smaller cells. Each is five-sided and at the juncture of two sides there is a small hair or hook. The cells appear to use this hook to join together. This could be the mode in which they grow. I was unable to determine what or how they eat. But, I guess since they are foreign and unique, they eat whatever they need to sustain their growth. Notice the successive slide of female #1. The five-edged organisms grow in sets of five. Five basic cells hook up to form a larger five-sided cell. This cell seems to pause. I suspect to consume nourishment. During the nourishment stage the five components transform into one. Then it seeks out similarly sized five-sided cells to create the next stage. None of this is visible in the root."

"Then the root is just a root?"

"I don't know. I am not a botanist, but what I do see is strange. Initially, the cross section appeared to be fibrous. Wood. Upon closer examination, I can see indications that this root has cell structure similar to ours. But not exactly like ours. Whatever the root is or to whatever it was attached, the thing is truly a hybrid. That makes it special. I'm going to call a colleague who is botanist, and get him to look at one of my samples. But, I found no five-sided cells and there appears to be no dynamic growth as noted in the blood. I question if this root had anything directly to do with the illness that infected Becky and Twyla Glee. Maybe Barry can find something more with his machinery. Maybe my botanist friend can shed some light on this mystery. I'm going to take several cross-sections from other areas. For the time being, gentlemen, that's all I know. I'm sorry I can't confirm what you suspected. But, the facts are the facts."

"Why don't we look in on the women?"

The return trip is sullenly silent.

"Boys, Isaac and I have decided we need to sit with the women in shifts. That way we can have someone here all the time and still take care of the farm. Each shift will be six hours, because there are four of us. Isaac will take the midnight to six watch. He hardly sleeps anyway. Aaron, do you have a preference?"

"I'll sit first thing in the morning… six to noon."

"Michael, you sit noon to supper."

"I'll relieve you at six. If anything happens while you are here, call Isaac or me right away. Is that clear? That's important because you will be here during the doctors' rounds. Ask them questions. Try to learn if anything has changed. Because it's now 4:30, I'll start the watch, by sitting from now until midnight. Isaac will relieve me. Dr. Hoffman has told me that we should know something in a day or two."

"Aaron, I'm going home with Neen."

"Suit yourself. I have some errands to run anyway."

"Grandfather, where did you get that root?"

"From the shaft in the Tal the first time we were there."

"Now, I remember seeing roots on your table. There were two. What did you do with the other one?"

"Nothing yet. I'm going to take it to Vincent this evening. Let him examine it from his perspective. I think the root is very important, and it's just that modern technology is not equipped to deal with things outside of their realm. The doctor in the lab has been trained to look at situations in a certain way. His examination was limited by his traditional training. That type of training does not restrict Vincent. He can look at the root, and, understanding its source, he can determine what it is and what it means. Do you want to go with me this evening?"

"I'd like to, but I have some things to do around the farm. Animals need tending before night fall, and I'm the boss tonight."

Michael checks the chicken coops to make sure that food and water are available. The roosters are strutting around. They puff their chests and crow mightily as they seek willing mates. He'll have to cull the flock tomorrow morning. On his way back to the barn, Michael checks the salt licks.

For the morning milking, all the hoses are clean and clear. He switches on the pumps one by one. They are ready. Feed is put into the trough. Normally this is done in the morning, because the feed dries overnight. But he will be alone tomorrow. Upstairs, he checks the electric fence connections, and turns the system off and on. His routine is completed. He heads for home and his dinner. During all the commotion, lunch was missed.

"Hi, Michael."

"Hi, Mary Ruth. You startled me. I didn't hear you drive up."

"How's your mother and Twyla Glee?"

"We don't know. They're at the hospital and under good care. We have to wait. Just wait. I don't like waiting. How did you hear about them?"

"I have my sources. Where's your dad?"

"He's sitting at the hospital."

"Where's Aaron?"

"Off running errands, he says. I suspect he went to see his buddies. But, he'll be home later. If you want me to have him call you, I will."

"No, that won't be necessary. I really came to see you and see how you were holding up."

"I'm OK, I guess. I mean I feel sorry about mother and Twyla Glee, but there's not much I can do about their illness. That's up to the doctors. I can be there and talk to them and give them support as they recover. Plus, I have to spend a little more time with the farm."

"Is there anything I can do to help you?"

"I can't think of anything off hand. I really appreciate the offer, but I think I'll be OK."

"Michael, what do you think of me?"

"That's a strange question. You're a friend of mine from school. You're a pretty girl. That's about it."

"Do you ever think of me any other way?"

"What do you mean?"

"Remember the night at my folks' house when I was taking care of your wounds and we kissed? I like the way we kissed. Did you like it?"

"Sure, I liked it."

"How did it make you feel?"

"That's personal, Mary Ruth."

"I know, that's why I'm asking. I'll tell you how I felt, and then you tell me how you felt. OK?"

The boy's silence is perceived as a tacit agreement.

"I felt all warm inside and a little light-headed. I wanted to kiss you more. I wanted to do more. I wanted to feel you and have you feel me. Then that damned Jimmy interrupted us. Now you tell me."

"I was nervous and confused. My body was reacting through the pain. I knew what could happen was not right. I was glad Jimmy returned."

Her eyes flare. She reacts to the challenge. Mary Ruth takes Michael by the shoulders and kisses him hard. To no avail she tries to insert her tongue between his sealed lips.

"What in hell are you afraid of?"

"Nothing. But, I don't like your attitude or language."

"Is it my language that turns you off or are you just too stupid to see what's in front of you and what is inevitable?"

"I know what you want. It's just that's not what I want."

"Are you gay?"

"No. I'm just not ready to do what you want."

"Then let me do it for you."

Mary Ruth unbuttons her blouse.

"Give me your hand."

"No. This is wrong. I think it's time for you to leave."

"You are pathetic. I had hoped you would want to fulfill your dreams about me. But, no, goodie two shoes wants to save himself. For what? For your wedding night? Get real, Michael. The only people who save themselves are priests and nuns and I'm not too sure about them. I can't believe you're rejecting me. No one rejects me."

She is yelling, pacing, and gesticulating in accelerating stages.

"Do you honestly think you can refuse my wishes? If you don't do what I want tonight, you'll be sorry. I got Jimmy and you to do what I wanted, and then I got back at Gene for not doing what I wanted. I got him and his dumb buddies real good. I have a little more work, and then Jimmy will be taken care of. And, I swear I'll get you, too. Who the hell do you think you are not to do what I want?"

Michael is dumfounded. The night with Jimmy, Mary Ruth, and Gene Dracal flashes back in puzzle pieces. The tears, the fight, Margaret's comments, the crash. The images flicker in no particular order. There is no single clear image.

"What are you saying?"

"I've said enough. It's time for action, and there certainly isn't any here."

"I'm going to walk you to your car, and you're going to leave. I don't believe what I heard. Your anger is so great that you would think about killing people who don't do what you want. Kill them. Do you have any comprehension how grave that is? Mary Ruth, I think you need professional help."

"Right now, I need you to pleasure me. Those boys died in an accident. If the stupid cops press the investigation, who would believe that a defenseless girl disconnected the brake line and bled it dry. That's more likely the action of a big mean boy like Jimmy. A boy, who carries a gun along with his tools in his lock box."

"Get in your car and leave."

"You have no idea what you are missing. Being with me would open doors to the greatest pleasures. Besides, it's your word against mine. In that kind of a fight, women always win, asshole."

The pebbles and dirt thrown by the spinning tires don't sting as much as the truth.

Hot water from the showerhead beats upon Michael's head and cascades over his body. Washing the farm and Mary Ruth from his body is ritualistically easy. But, he can't rid himself of what he must do. He must tell father the truth about what happened to Gene. Mary Ruth got into Jimmy's lock box and did the evil deed. Now she's trying to blame him for six deaths. Why is she so twisted?

Still wet, with the towel wrapped around his waist, Michael goes to the attic and climbs onto the roof. His moist footprints mark his ascent. Once in a great while he goes to this special space and thinks about things, which are heavy on his mind. He only goes at night. There are no lights at Neen's house. The glow of town lights is fast fading in the face of the oncoming black clouds. There is only one thunderhead, but it takes up the entire horizon. And it is moving fast, as if it has a purpose. The lightning is roiling behind the clouds, like guns at the beginning of a battle. The first bolt hits the Tal. Then another. And another. Until he can't count. It's almost like a machine gun. Every bolt lands somewhere over the hill in the Tal. He tries to peer over the hill. The towel falls at his feet. The flashes display his masculine form. Muscles flex and ripple with each strike. He is not afraid of being struck. Moisture from the shower mixes with the rain drops and coats his body. It glistens. His body reflects each bolt of light. Michael reaches his hands to heaven in supplication.

"What must I do?"

The horn from Aaron's truck shatters the intensity of the moment.

"What the hell are you doing up there? Get off before you're hit by lightning or you slip and fall. And, where are your clothes? Are you crazy? Dad would love to see this. His wife and daughter at death's door and his baby standing buck naked on the roof talking to the lightning."

SHERIFF

Michael's mind is spinning. So many bizarre events in the last few weeks, and they seem to be getting stranger and stranger. What's going on? What does this all mean? What should he do? What can he do? The moisture on his body is now the sweat of anxiety. His eyes, unblinking, are focussed on the expanse of his bedroom ceiling. Shadows take on reality. They slide and dance. Suddenly they are distorted by the appearance of a light from outside. The crunching of the driveway stones confirms that a vehicle has arrived at the back of the house. Father? Michael wants to talk to him. Explain things. Seek his guidance. The lights and engine are not turned off. The dinging of a bell tells him the vehicle door remains open. Michael hears the crackling of a police radio, then a pounding on the back door.

"Yes sir. What's the problem?"

"The problem is you, young man, and the assault of Miss Mary Ruth Martin. You'll need to come to the station with me. So get dressed. I'll wait in the cruiser."

"Michael, what does fat butt Gingrich want? What's he doing here?"

"He wants me to go to the station. He wants to question me about something to do with Mary Ruth."

"What about Mary Ruth?"

"She told the sheriff that I assaulted her this evening. She must have left here and gone directly to the sheriff."

"You mean she was here and you admit to that?"

"Yes, I have nothing to hide, because nothing happened."

"It'll be your word against hers. And that's not a fair fight when it comes to a girl's virtue."

"I've got to go with the deputy. Don't tell Father anything. I'll straighten it all out when I get back."

"If you get back."

The silence in the cruiser is interrupted only by the chatter of Paul, the night dispatcher.

"Sit here. Would you like a soda or some water?"

"No sir, I'm fine. I want to know why you brought me here when you could have asked me questions at the house like you did before."

"Miss Martin filed a complaint. I filled out forms and she signed them. By law, I must pursue a complaint of this nature with reasonable dispatch. That means tonight. I must determine if the compliant has sufficient merit to produce an arrest. The only way I can do that is to question the accused. Then I turn over all the information to the County Prosecutor. Then it's up to the County Prosecutor to determine if indictment and trial are the proper courses of action. The formal complaint means the form must be entered into the county files. To properly respond to the formal complaint, this office must investigate and complete another form, which is also filed with the county. If I don't follow the procedures, I am guilty of dereliction of duty. So, I'm just doin' my duty. There, now you know everything there is to know about police work. All the necessary forms are here, so we are here. Besides, I've found people tell the truth more often in this room than they do in the security of their home. The surroundings here bring out the best in people."

"If all you wanted was the truth, all you had to do was ask. I want to get this mistake cleared up so I can get home."

"Good, I like cooperation. Now tell me what happened between you and Mary Ruth?"

Michael relates all the details of his encounter with Mary Ruth, his feelings and responses, and her violent reaction. The deputy transcribes the monologue on the form…with a back-up sheet of paper.

"So, that's your side of the story. Unfortunately, it doesn't jibe with what the young lady told me. So, I am not sure your way is the way it really happened."

"I have no idea what Mary Ruth told you, but what I just told you is the truth. And, I've got something to say about what she told me when we were in the barn tonight."

He relates Mary Ruth's view of events of the night he went to Gene Dracal's house and points out the similarities of that evening and this.

"So, what you're saying is that she is guilty of setting-up both Gene and you. You say that she wanted you to retaliate against Gene because he spurned her. But, she says she asked you to go there and just talk to him. You say she wanted you to do more than just talk. She says you tricked her into going into the barn and tried to force yourself upon her, tearing her blouse in the process. But, you say she's retaliating against you because you spurned her. The two sides of the two events are pretty far apart young man. The young lady's makes sense. And, frankly, yours is pretty far-fetched. The critical point is the question of who spurned whom. And, we can't talk to Gene, can we? So, it's your word against hers."

"Margaret Eisenbaugh was the only one of the girls who stuck up for Mary Ruth, when I asked Gene what had happened. The other girls said nothing. I know Margaret lied. I know the other girls at the party won't confirm Mary Ruth's version of the events. They'll confirm Gene's version. They'll confirm the truth. That Mary Ruth approached him, not that he grabbed her. She attacked him, and he pushed her away. He spurned her, and she left before her clothes were ripped. But, her clothes were ripped when she got to Jimmy Hauck's. Jimmy'll tell you that. Since all that is true, then she lied to cause my confrontation with Gene. She lied to get me to get Gene. Since that's true, then you could believe that she could run to you, and file a complaint against me, although I did nothing wrong, except tell her I was not interested in what she wanted to do. She lied to you to get to me, just like she lied to me to get to Gene. She filed a complaint with you, just like she filed a complaint with Jimmy and me. Both complaints are based on lies. It seems that if she doesn't get her own way, she blames somebody else. And that her lies have grave consequences."

"What you're saying can be checked out. I'll talk to the other girls at the party. In the meantime, I suggest you stay away from Mary Ruth."

"There's something else."

"What's that?"

"The accident that killed the boys."

"What about it?"

"It wasn't Jimmy, who bled the brake lines. It was Mary Ruth."

"How far do you want to push this? First you claim the girl is guilty of lying and now murder?"

"I want all the truth to be known. I have no fear of the truth. Jimmy told me you checked his truck. You probably checked the lock box and the tools inside. Did you check for fingerprints? If you did, you'd find Mary Ruth's on the lock box and the tools, because she used the tools. Jimmy says he fell asleep when I left the truck. He had been drinking a few beers that night and he dozed off. That was Mary Ruth's opportunity to get her revenge for Gene's rejection. Maybe she just wanted to do some damage to his precious car. But, she is responsible for the accident. She told me that tonight when she came to the barn. I don't think she meant to kill anybody, just punish them."

"Well, now you're playing detective like some Hardy boy. And you expect me to just merrily follow what you say and arrest Mary Ruth on your say-so. How do suggest we get her fingerprints to compare them to the ones we might or might not have found on the truck lock box? "

"Not on my say-so. I'm asking you to check the facts. If she was in the lock box and handled the tools that were used to open the brake line, then she is guilty. Jimmy is innocent. I don't know how you go about getting her fingerprints. I'm not a sheriff or a deputy."

"That's right. But, you're trying to act like one."

"Why won't you listen to me? Why are you in such an all fire hurry to protect Mary Ruth, when the truth is just the opposite?"

"Jimmy Hauck had means and motive. Those Hauck boys are evil tempered and bad. You had means and motive. You're a teenager and Mary Ruth is a nice looking little girl with a cute figure. It's as simple as your hormones took over your actions and she said no to you just like she said to Gene Dracal. You got pissed, just like Gene Dracal got pissed, and you became physical, just like Gene. Both scenarios are logical and fit the facts."

"No sir, they fit Mary Ruth's version of the facts. All I ask is that you confirm my story with the girls, and check Jimmy's lock box for fingerprints. Two things that will prove what I'm saying is the truth. Now, if you have completed your official form, please take me home."

"Not before your read the form and sign it, just like Miss Martin did."

"I won't sign anything without my father. Shall I call him? I'm sure he would be none too happy to be awakened so that he could come to the station and listen to what you have to say."

"It's not totally necessary for you to call him, just sign the form."

"I think I'll call my father."

"I'll take you home."

Michael is the last to come home that night and the last to fall asleep, but he is the first to rise. He has to start the chores before five, and make sure Aaron leaves to relieve Neen. Normally, farm life is routine. There is security in routine. It has been anything but routine the last few weeks. Security has been shattered. The routine is now onerous.

"Michael, do you need me to help with anything?"

"No Grandfather, I can manage. Father left me a list of things he wanted done this morning before he woke up. I can do all of them myself."

"I spoke to Dr. Hoffman yesterday and he said the second set of blood tests proved negative. All of us are clear. It's like I said. It's the roots that attacked the women, and the women alone."

"Grandfather, I mean no disrespect, but if the roots carried the virus, why didn't you get it. They've been in your house for some time and you've handled them. Why not you and why Mother and Twyla Glee?"

"That I can't answer for sure. Maybe it is like an allergy. Some people have it and some people don't. Like the bites of the black flies on Aaron and you. But, I think Vincent knows. That's why I came here. Vincent wants to meet with us tonight. By us, I mean me, you, and Ruben. He says he's sure he knows what has happened and what is about to happen. He's got all the facts. He needs to discuss them with us. I'll talk to Ruben this afternoon, while you're at the hospital. He needs to understand the importance of all the recent events, and what they mean to his family. He needs to understand what he must do to protect us all. That's all I can say for now. I have to meet with Vincent before I talk to your father, then we'll sit together. No time for a nap."

After the milk is collected, Michael lets the cows out to pasture, and he rides the fence to check for breaks. He notes nothing out of the ordinary on the protective structure as he traverses the upper hill. Section nine is secure. It looks like there was some animal up here recently. The grass is depressed in one six-foot circle like a big dog or a wolf was curling around before lying down. It's part of their nature from thousands of years ago; they spun and matted the tall grass to create a resting spot. They never soil this spot. Michael gets down from the tractor, and walks to the circle to see if he can learn anything. No hair. No smell. And no track leading to or from the resting spot. Strange. It's like the dog just plopped out of nowhere, spun itself a resting spot, rested, and flew away. Like it was a watchdog. No reason to tell Father.

Back to the house for an early lunch. Hospital food is terrible and it's expensive. Better pack a sandwich for later.

"Good morning, Father."

"Hello, Michael. Say, did you hear someone last night? I thought I heard someone walking around after I was in bed."

"I got up to go to the bathroom during the night. It must have been me."

"No, I mean outside. It sounded like some animal or person was in the yard. But, I guess it could have been you inside. Or maybe I was dreaming about the dogs. When this mess is all over we'll get two more dogs. This time they'll favor your mother and me and not you children. You know, we're getting to the age when we miss the children we raised. Don't get me wrong, we love you three. It's just that you're all grown into adulthood and we miss the care and attention needed by little children. The dogs can be our next children. That's enough of sentimentality. Chores all completed?"

"Yessir. Now I want to shower so I don't smell in the hospital room. So, if you'll excuse me, I'll turn the care of the farm over to you, if you can handle it."

The smiles between the two generations spoke of love and the ability to tease. Bonds that time and distance couldn't shatter. Ruben takes his dishes to the sink to clean. Then he sits at the table and stares out the window, awaiting Michael's return. The back door opens with authority.

"Son, we need to talk."

"Isaac, what brings you up to the house?"

"I've been with Vincent and learned quite a bit more about a lot of things."

"Father, you and the professor or pastor, or whatever he is today are up to no good I'm sure."

"Son, this is serious. I can't go into the details, but we all have to meet with Vincent tonight."

"Father, I told you I don't want the boy's head filled with this nonsense any more. I hope I made myself clear on that matter. Because you believe what Vincent says, Michael does also. He trusts you. If Vincent is not right, neither of you will question him. It's particularly important that Michael stay focussed on his family and the farm until his mother and sister get out of the hospital."

"Ruben, what we need to discuss includes Michael's family and farm, but goes far beyond it. I ask only that you and the boy come to my house at seven tonight. Vincent wants to share with you all that he has learned. If, after the meeting, you don't agree with what he has to say, the matter is closed forever. But, if you agree that what he says makes sense, I will expect you will agree to do what needs be done."

"You're talking in circles, Father. But, out of respect, I'll bring Michael to your house after he gets home from the hospital. Aaron can go back and sit until someone else gets there. I'll tell him, when he gets in from the chicken coop. But just this once, then we are done with this magic stone myth. Is that clear?"

"OK."

The changing of the guard is not seamless. Aaron carps like any young man who is deprived of a night out with friends. Michael reports there has been no change in the condition of either patient. Dr. Hoffman seems pleased that their conditions have not deteriorated. The holding action seems to be working. He was on the phone to his friend at the CDC, and reports that their analyses of all the material are not yet complete. The experts are as mystified as everyone else.

"Father, I don't mean to be snippy, but I thought I was never to have any contact with Grandfather and the professor."

"All I can say is that sometimes your grandfather's will is more powerful than mine. He claims that Vincent has a great deal of important information to share with us. I can only assume the professor has learned the answers to the riddle of the stones. Maybe he has learned how to turn lead into gold."

"Now you're being snippy."

RUBEN

"Father. May we come in?"

"You don't have to be so formal. This is not the enemy camp."

"Professor, good evening."

"Good evening Ruben. Thank you for having a mind open enough to come here tonight."

"Sir, as I told Isaac, if all this still sounds like claptrap, Michael and I will leave and never speak of these things again. And, I would hope you would have the decency to do the same."

"That's fair enough. Let's begin shall we?"

"First, what about the stones?"

"Yes, the stones. They got me here to begin with. The black ones have a composition vaguely similar to the roots, which Isaac pulled from the tunnel. This connection convinces me they are from the same things. These are anthropomorphised evil spirits, who died a long time ago. This being true would explain the evil in the form of sickness, which they can generate. But, we'll get to that in a minute. The latter stones, the orange brown ones, which were turning color, have become totally black and are of the same composition as the other black ones and the roots. I believe these stones are fragments of spirits that died recently. When I say they died, I mean their spirit form was destroyed and they perished as animals or near-humans. The four multi-colored stones are special, and I believe they represent demons or demi-gods, which ruled the evil spirits. The fact that there are four stones is important to remember. But, I'll get to that shortly."

"At the very least this is far-fetched and mirrors ever-so-nicely the writings in the Book of Ancients. Like an interpretation of a myth by the mythmaker. I mean no animosity, sir, but we have no other source of information to confirm or refute your point-of-view. But, please go on."

"Son, don't be snippy and disrespectful of Vincent."

"Now the building in the Tal? I am convinced from all the physical evidence we have been able to gather that this was a place of religious ceremonies and rites. And, that remains such today."

"A church?"

"Not to our way of thinking. It is more of a temple of a religious sect by the standards of the day. A day long ago. The structure is solid as if it were carved from the huge stone protrusion in the earth. The same stone in which the shaft is mined. The hand of man builds churches stone by stone using mortar or plank by plank using nails. But there are no mortar seams in this building. And no nails. I doubt it would have been possible for man to carve this Keep. A project like that would have taken hundreds of men at least fifty years. Like a miniature pyramid. Slaves built the pyramids, but the settlers to this world had no slaves. They barely had enough men to protect their small villages. If the date in the family bible is accurate, the Keep would have been established before 1666. There were no settlers inland from the Atlantic Coast in time to build the Keep, so the Keep was not man made. Now the name above the door... ***Berg Alle Gotten***, means, "Keep for all the gods". Therefore, whoever worshipped at this temple believed there were many gods. This was a safe place for pantheism and pantheists. The religious sects that settled in this part of the New World were anything but pantheists. They believed strictly in one god. Therefore, it is safe to say that the building in the Tal could not be associated with the Dunkards, Pilgrims, Quakers, Amens, Mennons or any the splinter sects, which may have preceded them. It had to belong to some other group, which was completely different from them. Yet, the words above the door are in a language spoken by the people of the day. This leads me to believe that whoever worshipped in the Keep was aware of where they were and what or who their neighbors were. They may have tried to blend in by using the language of the area and time."

"You make it sound like a ghost castle, but a ghost castle of evil. If it belongs to a ghost, which is not real, then it is not real. Since it is real, there can be no ghost."

"Evil prevails in the Keep. The altar was and is a place of sacrifice. Real blood letting. The bowl in the middle of the altar top collects most of the blood. My assumption is that the priest and the worshippers drink the blood. That blood not consumed is allowed to run into the trough cut in the altar and down the back of the stone to the shaft cut deep into the mountain. I don't think this is a form of waste disposal. Rather, the blood, which ran down the shaft, is meant for some thing, which resides in the mountain. A gift or a feeding of some sort."

"What do you think is sacrificed on the altar?"

"Anything living and foreign to the worshippers. Small animals. Humans."

"Human sacrifice? You've got to be kidding. Why humans?"

"Humans outsiders. Outsiders are perceived as threats to the worshippers. Outsiders have to be sacrificed. The leaders demand it."

"This sounds like somebody trying to act like devil worshippers. Some wacko group like the one that killed the pastor. Maybe the same gang."

"There is no human gang here, because the Keep is not used by humans. I made the sign of the cross on the altar and on one of the floorboards the first time we were there. When we returned, the crosses had seemingly burned into both the stone and the wood. Obviously those materials reacted strongly to the marks."

"How did you make the sign of the cross?"

"With water."

"There you are. Oxidation. A simple explanation."

"Ruben, oxidation on stone maybe. A stone heavy with iron ore. But, rust on wood? Not likely. Besides, the rain, which falls in the Tal, would have oxidized, and there was no sign of that chemical reaction. The water I use is special. I have a small supply of water from the Garden of Eden."

"Sir, the Garden of Eden? Please."

"Many scholars believe the Garden of Eden remains, although in a greatly altered and deteriorated condition, in southern Iraq. Even the Iraqis consider the place sacred. Christians hold the River Jordan where John baptized Jesus to be sacred. Few of us have been fortunate to have samples of the water from both places. I am one so fortunate. It is the water from the Eternal Spring in the Garden of Eden that I used to bless the altar and the wood. These crosses are visible. They turned black, as if the water burned the surface and left a charred reminder of its presence. The water left scars on the stone and wood as if they were battle scars."

"You are stretching my intellectual tolerance and good nature, but go on."

"By understanding that this building is the house of evil, we understand a great deal."

"Professor, I will listen, but your connections are tenuous at best. It's just an old abandoned building, built centuries ago. Because it is strange to us, we fill it and our minds with superstitions. We make up stories about it to suit our fears and ignorance. And, over the years, these stories are embellished by people who don't like the fact that the truth is boringly simple."

"Perhaps it is simple, but it is never boring. When your father and I went back to the Keep the other night, we collected numerous items that corroborate the facts of the building. Before we get to those items, let me tell you about the shaft. It, like the building, is cut in solid rock. And, I suspect it is deeper than humans could plumb. I'll let Isaac tell you of his experiences."

"Ruben. Michael. I don't make up tales. When I went into the shaft the first time, I removed a few roots from the wall. They were black and gnarled. They vaguely resembled long fingers. Fingers that had lost their fingernails. Fingernails like the black stones. These are the same types of roots Becky and Twyla Glee handled. The things that made them sick. These new fingers without nails were taken from the evil tunnel. It's the evil in the tunnel that the fingers carry forth into the world to make people sick. When I went back into the shaft, I went deeper and saw a few more roots. I saw what I think were cats or huge rats. But, I never got a real clear look. The shaft was smooth, like it had been carved. I saw black stones on the wall that absorbed light just like the black stones you found when you were in the Tal, Michael. I also found a few stones that were different colors. Different from the ones you found. The smell within the tunnel was fierce. Smelled like sulfur and like rotten flesh. And the temperature changes were extreme and became violent. First the air was warm, and then got hot, and then it was cold. Then the temperature seemed to change by air current. One place it was hot as August. Two feet away it was cold as January. And I heard a noise that sounded like water, or birds or bats, but there was no screeching and nothing flew past me. So it had to be water. It must have been a half-mile away from where I'm hanging by the rope. A half-mile through solid rock is too long a tunnel to be carved by man. The tunnel was built by something other than man. When we got back, we examined all the stones… the ones Michael found and the ones I removed from the tunnel. The black ones were all alike. They absorb light. The colored ones all twisted light. But they were different colors. Vincent believes they are different demons from the original four."

"Fine. Allow me to offer logical explanations to this little fable. First and foremost, how is it possible that Becky and Twyla Glee contracted some mysterious virus from roots that you have been handling for a number of days? The fact that you did not contract the hemorrhagic fever from the roots is proof that the virus did not come from the roots. Unless, and here is a real leap of faith, unless the roots know whom to infect and whom not to infect. That makes no sense whatsoever, because the roots, like the stones, are inanimate… dead. They can't think or react. Now, on to your adventures. The tunnel is natural like the shaft in a volcano. We see tunnels and shafts in the earth all the time. This one is simply the largest one we've ever seen in this part of the world. The central part of a long-dead volcano. The fact that it is smooth is testimony to its age. Time does that to rocks. A volcano shaft also explains the smell, the noise, and the temperature changes. The bottom of the shaft is an opening above some fluid and changing strata of the earth. Any geologist will confirm this. Isaac, I mean no disrespect, but all your experiences while being lowered into the shaft are driven by your desire to see the mystical. You want to see a large rat. You see a shadow out of the corner of your eye. That becomes large rat in your mind. Like a child, who fears goblins under the bed. When the child looks, the goblin escapes. You want to find strange stones, and, by golly, you do. That these stones have similar properties to those found by my son is to be expected. Those stones are the models used by your imagination, which has been fueled by Vincent's pseudo-scientific-quasi-religious mumbo jumbo. So far all you have told me is gobbledygook wrapped in convenient rationale. I'm not angry, because this is beginning to sound humorous. I almost feel sorry for you. Don't you feel silly?"

Vincent is calm and he persists.

"Now to the names we found on the plaque at the Keep and in the bible. The fact that these are the same names ties your family to the building and its history. The five names, Mihai, Genber, Chzrut, Trelech and Nooem, are ancient. Four are listed below Mihai on the page from the bible, while these same are ranked above and separate from Mihai on the plaque. This obviously confirms that they are from different sects or environments from your family. This difference is the key. The four are the names of angels who, along with Satan, were banished from heaven by God after Michael and his host of archangels defeated them. Mihai is an ancient name for those whom we call Michael today. The Mihai on the plaque and the bible page was a member of your family. He was considered to be a protector. He fought and killed the four, who were worshippers at the Keep in the Tal. These four were worshippers of evil. They are represented by the four stones recently found by Michael. You will see in a few minutes, the time of the events is as important as the events themselves. These four were more than just spirits; they were four generals in the legion of the damned that belongs to the Devil… Satan."

"Slow down, if you please. I must lend the voice of reason, before the story telling gets too far. It is a very convenient happenstance that Michael finds four brightly colored stones and that four names appear in the family bible and on the plaque. Do the names also appear on the four bases of a baseball diamond? Why not the four Horsemen of the Apocalypse? What about the four seasons? I think we should look at all these facts from every possible angle."

"I ask that you listen a little while more. Now about the Tal. I did some digging into old deeds and records. And I learned that there is no deed for the land of the Tal. No one owns it. Not even the county. It seems to exist off the records. And in all the county's published lore and writings, I found only one very old mention of the name of the Tal…Naast. Naast is an arrangement of the letters in Satan. The Tal of Satan has existed since before there was a county with a government and records. It seems to have fallen through the legal cracks. The bible page and the plaque obviously do not recount the battle for superiority in heaven. They recount an earthly battle between the forces of good, as represented by Michael, and evil, represented by the four others. The fact that these four not only killed Michael, but were also killed by Michael during this battle on earth confirms that the metaphysical struggle did not end in heaven. The evil of the place and its unimaginable force in the cosmos are why the Tal and its name do not exist in any records. No one wanted to admit it existed. Maybe they felt like little children, if they ignored it, the evil would either not exist or it would go away."

"Now the Tal. The fact that this small piece of land is not on the county records means absolutely nothing. I am sure there are many places throughout the state and nation that are not platted. Maybe sections of land as large as twenty-five acres. Do we really know the true size of the Grand Canyon or the Appalachian Mountains, or our own county? A foot missing here and a foot added there, and soon we have an extra acre. The entire Tal, valley and hills, can't be more than two acres. Probably less. Given the size and complexity of this particular county, this amount of land could easily be off the books. I'm not positively sure where my land ends and my neighbor's begins. He and I are pretty sure, but not positively sure. If I farm three feet of his property or he mine, who knows? Once the Tal was lost no one cared until you, Professor. As to the name: Who knows for sure what the name of uncharted land really is? The name is what a generation says it is. And that name, because it is part of verbal history and not on the legal records can change with each generation. Our name is Hess, but around 1750, it was changed from Hesse. Name changes for immigrants are common. The name Naast is what it was called centuries ago. Today it has no name. You say that is a reconfiguration of Satan. Why not Santa? Or Stana? Or Tanas? Or maybe, in previous generations, other letters were added to or taken from the name, and they were lost by people who didn't care."

"Or maybe the people were afraid to say the name, Satan, because they didn't want to invoke him. So they rearranged the letters. Centuries ago, people feared calling a demon by its name, so they altered their reference to it. They also felt that great blasphemies would occur by the use of God's name, so they tried to avoid this in their curses by saying things like 'Sblood' and 'Sanger' for 'God's Blood' and 'God's Anger'."

"Speaking of names. You have put forth an interesting little Passion Play based on a parallel of myth and a splinter of vague history. Are we to believe that the four people were named for angels, who fought for power in heaven, lost and were banished to earth with Satan? This assumes substantial levels of physicality: First there is a heaven; second, there were or are angels that have form; third, there was a war or battle; fourth, the losing side left heaven; fifth, the losers came to earth; and sixth, the losing side came to this space we know as the Tal. Oh, and let's not forget that these angels continue their battle with the same angel, Michael, who vanquished them from heaven. Circular logic is a confusing argument. You just stretched the taffy and it broke. I would rather believe that these five people, most likely men, had names that had been handed down from the ancients. Names we don't use today. Probably like many of our names today won't be used four hundred years from now. One of these men was from our family and the four others were from other families. They entered into a dispute over land, water, or whatever. Our relative is given credit for killing the four. I am willing to believe there were others on the side of our relative. But, he may have been the leader, and his name is noted in our bible and on their plaque. Others who may have died in the struggle are not noted, because they were not significant. It's that way in wars. So, the war was not a continuation of the war in heaven it was an earthly event, among earthly people, who suffered the earthly consequence of war…death. There is no Tal of Satan and there were no fallen angels. It's as simple as that."

"Let's examine your family's bible further. On the torn-out page, it notes that the deaths from the original earthly conflict occurred in1666. Going through the family history, we can see that there are deaths on the same date in every century. On June 6 of 1706, 1806, and 1906, a male family member by the name of Michael died. Isaac confirmed this last one. Ruben, you may have heard of the Michael who died on June 6, 1906. It is more than happenstance that men with the same name died on the same dates for four centuries. The significance of the sixth day of the sixth month in a year ending in six must be acknowledged. St John's book of Revelations tells that the mark of the Great Beast is 666. Every man from your family who died on these dates was named for the angel, who expelled Satan from heaven. I think the evil beast was and is seeking revenge for his expulsion. And, the way these Michaels died is recorded in the bible as a heinous accident or some form of cataclysm of nature. Or so the people of the time thought. Look at this. One Michael tripped while chopping trees in the woods, he fell on his axe, and wolves ate him. Another drowned in the stream where the depth was less than three inches. The Michael, who died in 1906, was trampled by cattle, which had been attacked by buzzards."

"These are just freak accidents. The last Michael happened to be in the wrong place at the wrong time. It was tragic, but it was an accident. If these Michaels were or are angels, why or how were they killed? Weren't they protected by God?"

"As you can see from later entries, these men were married and had children. They were human. They had been with women. They weren't pure, because they did not represent the purest nature of man. Therefore, they could not compete with or defend themselves against the power of evil. Tomorrow is June 6th of 2006. Is Michael ready?"

Ruben can't deal with this question. He is stunned into rigidity and his words are soft and slow.

"You are suggesting that my son is an angel, who is supposed to fight and conquer the Devil. You say he happens to be in the right place at the right time. I say he is a boy and I won't put him in the wrong place at the wrong time. I won't put him in harm's way. If angels can fight against and defeat Satan's army, how do you explain the fact that Mihai died fighting Trelech and his band?"

"First, there is no way we can determine how many angels were involved in the original battle in the Tal. We only know those who died. It is safe to assume there were more than four evil angels and one pure human in this battle. We can further assume that Mihai was the leader, as Michael was the leader in heaven. We can go beyond that point and believe that Satan wants to inflict his revenge on all the Michaels, because they carry the seed of the one who killed Satan's four beloved generals."

"That's very convenient circular reasoning. Were there not other Michaels in the family tree? Why were they not killed by Satan?"

"Yes, Michael is a popular name in your family. Most did not die at the hand of Satan. None of them died on the dates in question and all died of apparently natural causes. Most died during sleep. It is only on these dates that these Michaels died violently. These additional notations are curious. The entries mention severe weather preceding the untimely deaths. In one instance there was a freak draught during the months of April and May. In another, there were hailstorms on June fourth and fifth. But, most often the entries mention powerful and persistent thunder and lightning storms with only a little rain. Not real rain storms."

"Grandfather, I thought the storms we're seeing now occur every year."

"They do. Some years are worse than others are. This is one of the very bad ones. In all my years, I can't remember a worse one."

Ruben stares straight at the far wall and sits uncomfortably silent. He fears this line of discussion is going to a bad place for his son. He has been frustrated by Vincent at every turn. And that he is powerless to stop what Vincent and Isaac want.

"Your father told me there have been several unexplained instances involving farm animals recently. Specifically, the flies and the Guernsey, the buzzards and the chickens, and the death of your two dogs. These are not aberrations of nature, which can be ascribed to the phase of the moon. These are probes. Satan is sending his minions to probe the farm and your family in forms, which we see as earthly. His goal is to determine where is his tormentor, Michael. The Guernsey was lured up the hill and slaughtered so you would find it. The flies were there not so much to harm you, but to report to Satan. Aaron became infected by the evil, just as your wife and daughter. Buzzards never attack live animals and they never attack at night. Yet these did. Yes, you drove them off, but they learned about the family and your son. The dogs were killed so that you would know the evil force was probing closer…from hill to flatland to barn. And the roots confirm it all. Isaac was not infected by the so-called hemorrhagic fever, because the Great Beast does not care about him. The Evil One wants to kill the source of his torment. He wants to kill the woman who gave birth to this Michael."

"Why, my son?"

"Because he is the living threat to the ancient dead. His name tells it all. Michael Abdiel Hess. His middle name means 'the pure one'. He is the warrior angel. He is the one whom Satan fears the most. Son, tell me, have you ever been with a woman?"

"No sir."

"He is."

Vincent's emphatic whisper echoes throughout the small house and deadens all other noise. Three generations of Hess men stare at the table, the open book, and each other. Their muscles sag from the emotional struggle to cope with the inevitable.

"Ruben, do you see? All of this makes sense. The Tal houses evil. An evil which has existed before time and has fought with our family for four hundred years. My grandson, your son, has the chance to rectify all of that. Before Satan can cause more earthly damage, Michael must confront him."

"If we accept all that has been said tonight, what do you expect Michael to do?"

"It's simple. Michael must go to the Keep in the Tal and do battle with the Great Beast. He must vanquish the Ancient Evil from earth, just as the original Michael vanquished him from heaven. Satan must be sent back down the tunnel in the Keep and it must be blocked so that he may not escape. The Keep must be destroyed."

"And, how will this happen?"

"Other than going to the Keep and confronting Satan, I have no idea what shape the battle will take. There will be participants other than Satan and Michael. Satan will try to seduce Michael with his power. Get him to believe. He will not be fair. Equity is not a quality of this battle. God will be there in some manner. Most likely in the clouds of the storm. He will ensure Michael's ultimate safety. The battle will not be a physical confrontation, because Satan chooses not to adopt a human form. His servants will appear to be human in Michael's mind. It will be a mental and emotional battle and Michael will be victorious if he does not go into the Keep. If he stays on the floor of the Tal and defeats Satan's emissaries, Satan will have to come out of the Keep to do battle directly. That's when God will intervene and crush Satan."

"You just said my son will be bait to lure Satan. How can you guarantee my son will not be harmed? And if God is there, why doesn't he do battle with Satan? The Devil's quarrel is with God, not my son. Why is God hiding behind a teenage boy? If this fight began in heaven, God should be the one to fight The Beast on earth."

"I have faith. God has chosen Michael to continue the struggle between good and evil. God has chosen Michael to represent all mankind. Michael and his actions will demonstrate that mankind can live a good and godly life under free will. He will choose not to be seduced by power. He will choose to remain true to God's way. This is the true test against evil."

"Free will? Your argument so far is that Michael has been chosen. Therefore, he has no free will. Now I mean disrespect. I am not putting my son's life in jeopardy based on your faith in predestination. We will go with him. I will go with him. Isaac will also go."

"By chosen I mean appointed. He can accept or refuse the appointment. He can exercise the free will that God gives for humans. He must be responsible for his actions. As to accompanying him? No. Only the pure may enter into battle. On one side, there is pure spiritual evil. On the other, there is pure human good with free will. Although you have free will, you are not pure because each of you has been with a woman. Purity is your son's ultimate shield against evil. It was the shield that protected the angels in heaven. If those who are not pure are with Michael, his army is not pure. If his army is not pure, he will fall victim to Satan. But, if he stands pure before evil and under the watchful eye of God, Michael will be victorious."

"What do you say will happen if Michael doesn't go to the Keep and fight? What if I forbid him to go?"

"Then the risk to him becomes a reality. Satan will leave the Tal and walk among us on earth until he finds Michael and destroys him in the most gruesome manner. A manner that will take time and be brutal. A demonstration of Satan's power. The only way to destroy the Devil is to go to him. Confront him in the Tal. The Devil will try to destroy the boy, but he will fail, because the God in heaven will protect Michael."

"How do you expect Michael to go to the Keep alone?"

"I didn't say alone. I said that you may not accompany him. I will be there. I have been celibate all my life. Plus, I have knowledge in these things. Knowledge which can help Michael during his time of trial. I will be his counsel. Not a warrior."

Ruben looks lost and alone. His eyes plead with his father. He feels as if he is a mouse in a maze. At every turn, Vincent demonstrates that Ruben's question is without merit. Vincent has a reasonable sounding answer for every question. Ruben feels he is dealing with someone, who has been through this maze before. Someone who knows which way Ruben will turn before Ruben knows.

"I need time to think about this."

"There is no time to ponder, we must act and make Michael ready for his battle. The lightning will commence shortly. It is God's sign to us that he is ready to protect Michael in the battle."

"Father, what if the professor is wrong? What if there is no Great Evil in the Tal? Suppose the evil is real…wolves or bears. They won't listen to metaphysical arguments. They will kill to live. To them it's basic."

"Don't be foolish. Vincent knows there are no wolves or bears in the Tal. Animals are the superstitious reasons behind questions people can't answer. If, as you believe, there is no Great Beast in the Keep, then you are right and all of this has been for naught. And nothing will happen to Michael. I will look foolish. But the evidence from all the sources is overwhelming. There is evil. It has caused substantial harm. We have a chance to defeat the evil. We must do so."

"But, there is also a great risk that destruction could befall my son. I don't want to lose him."

"Son, sometimes you have to trust and let go so that you may keep. Why don't you ask Michael?"

"Father, I know you want only what's best for me, but I believe what Vincent says. I believe it because I have seen much with my own eyes. I believe it because Neen believes it and he would not lie. So, now you have to let me do what I can. Tell me, would you do it? Would you go to the Tal and combat the Beast of Evil if you were in my place? I believe you would. If Neen's son were asked to exercise his free will, and based on the evidence and his faith in his son, Neen would say yes. I am frightened, but I have faith. I ask your approval for me to do this thing."

The total argument is too persuasive. At every turn Vincent has evidence, whether real or created to fit the events. It has convinced Ruben's father and son. Isaac believes the stranger and all his rationale. He is old and given to the old ways. With medicine, he thinks the old potions are better. He will not use manmade fertilizers. Vincent speaks of mysteries from the ancients. It is only natural that Isaac believes him. Michael is a young man who wants to believe the myths and magic of another world. It is reasonable to understand that he would believe Vincent. That leaves Ruben as the voice of reason. A voice silenced by a majority of believers. Ruben's head nods ever so slightly, his eyes blink, and a faint smile of humility in loss creeps over his lips.

"I can argue against this no longer. I will help as much as I can."

"Ruben, you will see. We will win."

TAL

Ruben calls the hospital, inquires about his beloved patients, and tells Aaron he will have to sit watch until some one relieves him. It won't be too long.

"Is everyone ready?"

"I guess."

"Before we head up the hill, be sure we know our duties. Ruben, you and Isaac will accompany us to the fence. After Michael and I are beyond the fence, you will close it and stand guard for our return. Do not follow us. Your presence in the Tal will jeopardize Michael's safety. We will go over the crest of the hill and into the Tal. The general timetable is an hour. If we have not returned by then, it only means that we are still in conflict. Do not worry. Michael and I will return. My guess is that the storm will come early tonight... before eleven. It will be the most powerful display of lightning so far, but there will be no rain. And it will probably last less than an hour. The lightning will stop in enough time for Michael and I to climb down the other side of the hill and be on the floor of the Tal a little after midnight, which will be the first hour of Michael's birthday...June 6, 2006. That's when the confrontation will commence."

"How can you be so sure that the storm will pass by midnight? The thunder and lightning usually start after eleven and then there's a lot of rain after that. The rain lasts for about two hours. Why will tonight be different?"

"Although the lightning is always accompanied by thunder and followed by rain, lightning is the only one of the three storm elements that matters. The other two elements are disguises for human eyes. God uses the lightning to hold Satan in his place; inside the Keep. God's power in the form of lightning could destroy Satan. By bombarding the Tal, God kills the evil minions of the Great Beast. They come from the tunnel in the Keep and roam the Tal each evening. When we have been on the floor of the Tal and in the Keep, each of us has sensed the presence of animal-like creatures flitting about. Maybe we've seen their eyes or some semblance of form scampering from darkness to darkness, just slightly out of our line of vision. Sometimes we thought they were wolves. Sometimes cats or rats. We may have even heard their staccato breathing, like an animal panting. These are the evil underlings that Satan wishes to send into the human's land to do his bidding. These are the spirits whom God easily kills every night with lightning. Remember the craters, which pocked the ground around the Keep? These are caused by lightning strikes. The stones and any roots, which may remain in the craters, are the remnants of the evil spirits. Those evil creatures, which could not make it to safety in the Keep or some other form of hiding when the bolts of lightning hit, are destroyed. Upon seeing the first bolt and hearing the first clap of thunderous rage, most of the creatures scurry back to the Keep and the passage to the netherworld. It infuriates Satan that most of his evil creatures are so cowardly that they run from God's first strike. So cowardly that they don't venture out of the Tal and do his evil bidding. But, he is pleased that every once in a while one or two of these spirits escapes the Tal and enters into the human world to do his destruction. He has millions of evil spirits... souls of those who chose Satan over God. And he has no concern about sacrificing thousands so that one or two can escape. Those, which he sacrifices, are easily replaced. Like disposable shavers. And, trust me; there is a never-ending supply of souls. Those who are brave enough to confront God in the name of Satan are special spirits. Closer to Satan than those who run tuck-tailed. These special souls walk like humans among humans and promote Satan's way."

"Are these the evil spirits that slaughtered our cow, attacked the chickens, and gutted the family pets?"

"Yes."

"How do they escape God's wrath?"

"Once out of the Keep, they have the ability to transform into ether and float unseen in the darkness of the tree and bush growth until the lightning is finished. But they have to be quick to hide this way. When God's wrath subsides for the evening, they transform to animal-like forms, come over the hill, somehow get through the fence with its physical and spiritual barriers, and wreak their havoc."

"Sir, I hear your words, but I'm not convinced that this plan is safe for Michael."

Six eyes stare at Ruben.

"My grandson will be fine. This is his destiny. Let's get a move on."

While one trudges, three walk briskly over the flatland. The lightning has started and the sound and light show is magnificent. Now that Michael knows that the bolts are like artillery barrages, in his mind he sees the Devil's minions scurrying around to avoid the fury from the sky. Like hundreds of rats on the barn floor and Michael has his .22. There are so many rats that the floor is an undulating gray mass with thousands of beady eyes. The faster he shoots, the more he kills. He doesn't really have to aim. Those not killed scamper back to their nest. A few escape the barn and run to the field to start new lives.

The lightning is showering down on the Tal. The bolts seem narrower and more pointed than before, and certainly there are more of them. Michael notices that some flashes are single colors. Reds. Greens. Blues. Yellows. Now a broad-spectrum cascading light splintered pillar with jagged edges crashes through the center of the narrow strikes. A second, wider than the first, hits right away. The boy has never been this close to the strike zone. Never this close to the fury and magnificence of the bolts. The peak of celestial bombardment is sustained for thirty minutes. It ends as suddenly as it began.

"Now we go. Ruben, be sure to close the fence immediately after we are through it. You and your father must wait on this side of the fence for us. Do not come into the Tal. Do not jeopardize Michael."

Two boards are pulled aside and two men slip through the opening. The boards are replaced as the human forms disappear up the hill. All is quiet. Ruben's watch indicates it is 11:35. They who wait also serve, but waiting is unnerving.

The watch shows 11:36. The two stare at the barricade and wonder.

"Father, did you bring your shotgun?"

"No."

"Don't you think you should have it?"

"Why?"

"In case one of the animal forms tries to get through the fence."

"You have yours."

"Yes, and I would feel more comfortable if you had your old double-barrel blaster."

"Don't you think one gun is enough?"

"Based on my experience with the buzzards, two are barely enough. Please, for my sanity, go back to your house and get your gun."

"What happens if…"

"Vincent said nothing would happen in the Tal until they got down to the Keep. If you hurry, you can be down and back before the real fireworks start. Now, please."

"OK, I'll be right back."

As the old man's shape fades into the pitch of shadows and long grass, Ruben writes:

Have gone to the crest. Signal me with flashlight when you return. It's better this way. I'll not lose my son.

He impales the note on one of the pulled nails, slides apart the boards, slips through, replaces the panels, and scampers up the hill. Serenaded by the thundering of his heart, he peers over the crest. The Keep looms foreboding in the center of the Tal floor. The moon reveals hundreds of craters on the floor. Ruben can't tell which were created tonight and which were created the nights before. Standing beyond the undergrowth are two human forms. The larger one has his hand on the shoulder of the other. The Tal is still except for the walking of two forms and brief rustling of undergrowth. Instinctively, he turns his gaze to the fence and spots his father's signal…a constant blinking. Ruben responds and both lights are extinguished. Shotgun at the ready, he steps over the crest to the other side. Into the arena.

"What do we do now?"

"First, I bless us with the most holy of waters. Crosses on foreheads, hearts, and hands. Then we wait to be confronted. It won't be long. Remember, you will think you see and hear things that seem real, but there is no physicality to what you experience. What you experience is what the Devil is communicating to you. It's like a dream he is putting in your mind. It does not exist in the world based on human ideas of time and space. And the second thing to remember is like the first. Satan is the Grand Deceiver. He has a plan. He knows what he wants. He wants to rule both heaven and earth. He is single-minded, and nothing will stand in his way. To get what he wants he has no issue against lying or killing or committing any of the man-named Deadly Sins. To him, the ends always justify the means. His ends are beyond your understanding, so his means will be also. The images and sounds with which he fills your senses are designed to convince you that you should side with him. That you should trust him. He will attempt to seduce you with his power…his might, and his twisted reasoning. If you believe the images and their words, you will believe him. If you believe him, you will not believe God. Then Satan has won this major battle. He has defeated God by converting another human to his side. You have converted, because you have chosen to believe Satan of your own free will, he has conquered you and nullified God's power without shedding a drop of your blood."

"How can I fight the images I see and the words I hear?"

"That's why I am with you. I am your counselor. As your medium, I am your eyes and ears to the real world. To free will and a right choice. When you see something, tell me what you see. When you hear something, relate the voices and the words exactly as you hear them. When you relate what you experience, I will be able to guide you to react in the appropriate manner. I am free of Satan's influence. He does not wish to conquer me. You are the target of his actions. But, it is your free will that makes the process possible. It is your free will that allows you to relate the sensations accurately, inaccurately, or not at all. It is your free will that allows you to take my counsel and fight the heinous wishes of The Beast, or ignore my advice and yield to his seduction. Soon he will send his messengers to do his bidding. He will emerge from the Keep when he has exhausted his envoys, because they are expendable. Or, when he thinks he has worn down your resistance. Then he will come out to the Tal's floor for the *coupe de grace*. He wants to claim his trophy in the sight of God. He will take your soul into the Keep. So you must resist him and rely on me."

Michael promises to let the experiences happen, relate them to Vincent, and rely on his counsel.

The mist in the doorway of the Keep stirs and begins to glisten in the moonlight. Slowly a shape becomes apparent. Mary Ruth. She steps from the Keep and gracefully walks toward Michael. A diaphanous pink cloth covers her from shoulder to ankles. The outline of her form is apparent. Her eyes are moist and her skin radiates. She is smiling warmly. Her hands are raised from her side, palms upward to embrace the boy.

"Michael, I'm so glad you came. I wanted to see you again after that unfortunate night. You know you missed the opportunity to be inside me. But, with me, you can always get a second chance. Let's kiss and forget about what happened. Think only of the pleasure that awaits you."

Her toga opens to reveal her teenage breasts and small firm belly. She places her hands on Michael's cheeks to kiss him. He grasps her shoulders, stops her approach, and pushes from his face.

"Resist her, Michael. She is a messenger of evil."

"No, Mary Ruth, no. What you want is wrong."

"Mary Ruth, will you come down here. Deputy Gingrich is here and he needs to talk to you."

"Mother, I'll be down in a few minutes. I'm just getting out of the tub."

The water is so hot that it has dulled her skin's senses. The bubbles in the bath have faded and she is visible beneath the surface. Why didn't Michael want what the other boys had? She reaches for the cutting blade she took from art class months ago and stares at it as if she expected it to perform her task. She rolls her left arm to expose the pale under side. Slowly and emphatically, she inserts the blade into the heel of her hand and tugs it three inches toward her elbow. The pain is negligible. Valium and two beers saw to that. The blood effuses from the gash, pours over the wrist, and streams into the bath water. The rich red becomes brown pink in the soapy water. Clots form. Mary Ruth rests her head on the end of the tub, closes her eyes, and awaits her fate.

"Dear, the deputy is waiting."

"Three minutes and I'll be dried and dressed, Mother. You wouldn't want me to come downstairs naked would you? Tell Deputy Gingrich he'll just have to wait."

In three minutes it will be too late to save her. Maybe it's been too late for too long.

The heat from the apparition's touch stings Michael's cheeks more than hurts. Mary Ruth is glowing like an ember. Her smile of pleasure has been replaced by a toothless grimace of pain. Her eyes are wide in panic. She staggers backward three paces and Michael sees a new female. This one is old and bent. Sores cover her flesh and the sores' ooze glistens. Her hands are gnarled. Clumps of hair are matted on her head. Beneath the red toga are flab

143

and flaps of flesh where before he had seen the beauty of a teenage body. She is writhing on the ground. Her appearance is no longer seductive. She resembles a Praying Mantis caught in a trap. Flailing viciously, but helplessly.

"Why, Michael, why? Why do you reject me? I am your pleasure here on earth. Come and fuck me. Or are you a simpering faggot?"

Her lilting and sensuous whisper has become a grotesque loud cackle. She is twisting and contorting, thrashing and shriveling. This former beauty is being reduced to an ugly mass of something alien. The protoplasm sinks into the earth.

"You did well, Michael. We are a good team. You passed the first test."

Ruben can see nothing except the two human forms. They seem to turn to each other occasionally as if in conversation. He peers over the crest to the fence and sees rapid blinking of a light. Isaac is angry. They cannot converse, and Ruben can not flash his light for fear some one or thing other than his father would see it. He sits beside the crab apple tree. Thoughts are whirling. Disjointed thoughts as if they were pieces of different jigsaw puzzles that he must somehow put together to form a new picture. Words, phrases, and images from various times and places hint that something is awry. Something is not as it is perceived. In the past, when he has had fragments of thoughts like these, he learned that something he thought to be right was wrong. Or, the answer to a nearly impossible conundrum became abundantly clear. Experience tells him to clear his mind and let it sort through the morass. He can't force any filters or restrictions on the process to solve the problem. In time, the pieces will come together. But, there is no time; there is only a real urgency. Ruben keeps hearing Vincent's words. Vincent had a quick and convenient answer for every question. He never once said 'I don't know', or 'I'm not sure' like everybody else might say. No one has the answers to everything. All his answers tied together to form one vast cohesive understanding of the situation. He seemed to be aware of the grand design, when all anybody could see were separate and disparate details. Maybe that's why he is an expert. Or did he know the design beforehand.

"That wasn't so difficult, Vincent."

"No first test is ever difficult if you're prepared. How do you feel?"

"Fine."

"Do you feel strong enough… do you have enough energy for more?"

"Sure."

"If you are thirsty, I have some more special holy water in my pack."

"No I'm fine."

"I suggest some water. These events are spiritually draining and this water will help you keep your acuity. It's right here."

"Thanks. I'm fine."

"Are you sure?"

"Yes sir, I am sure."

Michael's reading of the second chapter begins. From the side of the Keep step two humans. They walk a few paces from the building and stop. In the post-storm moonlight, Michael recognizes the Dracals.

"Michael, it's nice to see you again. I told you we would meet. Come here so we may speak in private."

"No thank you ma'am. I think I'll stay right where I am. I feel more comfortable here."

"Then you don't mind if we come to you."

"No ma'am."

Dr. and Mrs. Dracal step out of the building's shadow and gracefully cover the distance to Michael and Vincent. The doctor is in his familiar black suit, white shirt and black bow tie. His dark horn-rimmed glasses seem inordinately large on his ferret face. His skin is as pale as his shirt. Like he is bloodless. Mrs. Dracal is properly dressed in a maroon skirt and dark blue blazer. Her white blouse has front ruffles and a scarf tie. Her hair is severely pulled back and shines in the light. Her eyes are coal black and dead, but her skin radiates like Mary Ruth's. She is wearing four-inch stiletto heeled shoes that don't sink into the earth and she stands fully three inches taller than the doctor, who deferentially stands behind her.

"Well here we are. I'm pleased you have come to your senses and decided to let us help you. There is so much for us to teach you before you are ready to assume the mantle of leadership on earth."

"I am not here to learn from you. I am here to confront the source of all evil. God has chosen me and I choose to do battle with Satan. I will defeat him."

"Why in the name of all that is right would you want to imperil your frail existence by pitting your human body and soul against the greatest power in the universe? Why indeed would you fight the same power that offers you the opportunity to become the world leader and rule beside him in his eternal and infinite realm? Have you been listening to the lies of the fool by your side?"

"He is my counsel."

"Has your counsel explained why his God allows destructive things to happen to apparently good and decent souls? Has your counsel explained that this same God will ignore you if you do not do what he wishes? Has he explained that free will is nothing more than an excuse for God's failures? Has your counsel explained why this supposed all-powerful God has a little boy do his bidding? Why he hides behind a mere human? Why he fears his certain demise? Michael, you have been duped by a deceitful God and his lying emissary. We offer you the clarity of truth."

"I can choose to believe whatever I want. Free will is a gift from God."

"Listen closely to what I tell you. Imagine a government in power. When this government is in power, the people think it is good, because it is all they know. When the government is examined from an outside perspective, it is seen to be evil. When this government is overthrown, the people realize the old government was evil and the new one, the replacement government, is good. You have been told all your life that your God is good and Satan is evil. That book of lies was written by his followers, who feared him. Of course they wrote that he was good and all-powerful. What else did they know? How very convenient that those who fear God tell you that God is good. People, who can only view from one side, can only see what they are allowed to see. They are the people who follow God and fear another. Of course, your God has to tell you that Satan is evil. Because, without a perception of evil, the so-called good has no power or authority. What would you fear if there was no bogeyman? What would you cling to if there were no danger? Your God created the myth of evil. A universal and timeless perspective shows the truth. The truth is that your God is the deceiver. It is in his best interest to lie so that he may maintain control. Without control over his minions, he fails. Open your mind and realize that in the grand scheme of the universe, there are two sides to every story, and the truth can't be discerned from just one."

"What you say is interesting. You claim to have the real perspective. Why should I believe you? Why is my perspective wrong? Who is to say that your perspective is final? Why can't there be a point-of-view that confirms God is good? Why can't there be a time when the people realize the replacement government is evil and the old one was truly good; that they were deceived by evil into overthrowing good? Of course, there has to be evil as an opposite to good. Just as day counters night, and love counters hate. And, humans have the free will to choose which one they want. Choice outside our ken is based on faith. We must have faith to accept the teachings of a merciful and loving God. A God who has, throughout time, had one message…love. A God who has repeatedly demonstrated his undying love. He created a son and then sacrificed that son, so that we would understand, just how pure is God's love and how deep is his forgiveness. If love is pure, then hate is impure. God is love, so Satan is hate. God is pure, so Satan is impure. Impurity is essential to your existence. Your lord preaches self-centered domination of others. He preaches hate. Humans have the free will to choose. I choose love and God."

"You are a fool. Do you really think your God will let you sit at his table? Do you think the same God that banished my lord will accept a human as his child? He already sacrificed his son, who was human. What makes you think he will not sacrifice you? If you follow Satan, you will have power like no other man before you. If you follow Satan, you will rule at his side. You will rule earth as his equal. If you reject my lord, you anger him. Let me show you the power of my lord. Watch what I show you."

In the hospital room are Michael's mother and sister. His point-of-view is from between their beds. The monitors are beeping insanely. Pulse rates are 48 then 96, then back down to 39, then up to 120. Blood pressure readings for both patients match those extreme fluctuations. The temperature for both patients bounces from 92 to 104…from 89 to 106. The women are writhing in pain. Sweat is drenching their bedclothes.

"Michael, save your sister. Please Michael, be a good son. It hurts so much. Won't you help her?"

"If your acceptance of your God's lies and rejection of my lord continues, you can watch your loved ones die in incredible agony. Or you can acknowledge the power of my lord, and he will cure their illness and raise you to the level of leader. They will return to you, as you knew them before they fell ill. It's your choice."

"Choice is the real issue. The choice you and your lord offer is based on a threat. A condition. God's love is unconditional. Because he gave me free will, he knows that I am subject to errors and failures. His love is extended to me regardless of my actions. I can choose to accept it or not. I can choose to love or not. Satan's love is conditional. He will only love me if I love him first. Or, if I do something to prove my love. My free will means I always have a choice. I can choose to believe or not in the power of God. I can choose is to accept or not God's freely offered love. I choose to accept that love. I choose to believe in his power, because he does not threaten me with it, or threaten to take it away."

"You and your arrogance have condemned your mother and sister to a horrible death that will take weeks. Their agony can only be stopped by your rejection of the lies of your God and acceptance of the true lord of the universe, my lord."

"You do not have the power to do such a thing, because you are a pawn. God won't allow Satan to make it happen. God loves my mother and sister and he will not permit them to be used as the Satan's toys. He will defend them against any further onslaught, because this illness is not their choice."

With a simple, pronouncement of faith, Michael creates a silence. Vincent puts his arm around the boy's shoulders.

"Well done."

The glow comes from nowhere. Papers begin to smolder. Heat intensifies and suddenly there is a crackle of flame on the desk. It licks at the manuscripts and books. Dried by the years, they are natural kindling. Parchment becomes a torch to the wood. The flames creep across the desk and leap onto the chair. Then they spring to the wall shelves and begin devouring the knowledge of the ancients. Myths, legends, and twisted truths explode into a blaze that reaches the ceiling. The inferno consumes all the oxygen in the closed room. Suddenly the heavy black door explodes as the flames gasp the nourishment of oxygen. They slither along the floor and bound up the walls from the first to the second story. Within five minutes, the entire structure is burning. The heat is so intense that metal melts and marble crumbles. The Eden Valley FD has never seen such a fire. So fast. So complete. So intense. The Dracal house is ash in less than a half-hour. There was no stopping the inferno.

The male and female forms before Michael turn and head to the Keep. Halfway there, some force stops them. They are frozen in space. They twist to face their human adversary. Michael sees little puffs of smoke on their clothes and the nascent flickers of fire that follow. Mouths are open, but the forms do not speak or scream. Their eyes tell their entire story. They have failed, so they are expendable. The flames grow from two inches to twelve. They engulf the forms. Instantly their clothes and flesh burn away to reveal nothing. No bones. No structure supporting the exterior. A canvas upon which had been painted evil in the guise of human. In moments, all that remain are two small piles of ashes. These are dispersed by a gust of wind from the Keep. How easily Satan dispenses those who fail.

"Is it over?"

"I can't answer that. Only you will know for sure. Do you believe you have defeated Satan?"

"I doubt it. This was much more difficult than the first. But, I believe Satan has more tests for me. Now I am thirsty."

"Here drink my water."

"Thanks anyway, Neen made me some of his special tea for energy. I'll drink that."

"This water is what you need. I insist that you have some. It's pure and holy."

"I appreciate everything you are doing for me, but I'll stick to the tea."

"This water will replenish your spirit, because it is the water with which I blessed us. Here let me mix some with the tea."

"I told you, no thank you. Why are you trying to force your water on me? I don't like you telling me what to do."

"I demand that you follow my orders. Drink this water."

KRIEG

The pieces are bouncing around in Ruben's mind. Pastor Zug said Vincent had an eye for the co-eds, and they for him. Vincent said he had been celibate all his life. Pastor Zug had nothing to gain from lying. Was Vincent lying? If he was a lady's man when Pastor Zug first met him, there is a good chance Vincent was not celibate all his life. If he lied about that, what could he gain? What does he have to gain from any lies? He gained Isaac's confidence. This helped him gain Michael's confidence. First he conveniently explained the stones then he took them to the Tal as if he were on a scientific expedition. It was all a ruse to gain their acceptance. After that they would believe anything he told them. They believed him so completely they allowed Michael to go into the Tal tonight. And Ruben went along with it. He was duped, too. What was that phrase Vincent used…'he is'. It sounded like an amen. That's what was written in blood on the wall of the Pastor's house… 'Er ist'. It means 'he is'. He is what? No. It means he is. He exists. The Devil exists, and Vincent is the Devil's soldier. All his answers tied together too tightly. He knew the answers before the questions were asked. He had seen the picture and the plan before it was broken down into small human-sized pieces. He was the human's guide, who let Michael discover what he wanted Michael to see. This entire past few weeks has been scripted. Scripted by Satan. Scripted to produce a specific end. An evil end. And Michael is the sacrifice to that end.

The other word that Vincent uses was 'pure'. The family bible tells us that there is nothing as pure as the love between a parent and child…between God and man. Pure, because it is unconditional. Ruben's love for Michael is unconditional. Ruben's love is pure. Now all the pieces fit. He sees the total picture clearly. Ruben must get to Michael before Vincent and Satan can harm the boy. Clutching his Mossberg in his left hand, he starts down into the Tal. The lope quickly becomes a sprint. The leaves, twigs and branches are minor impediments. They scratch his arms, face and clothing. The humble workman is unafraid. The farmer begins to bellow like a bull. Nothing on earth is more powerful than a parent protecting a child. Nothing is more pure.

"Michael, be careful. Vincent is not what he claims. Run to me. Run up the hill toward the farm. Now."

He sees the two forms struggling. It's as if the larger is trying to force something upon the smaller. Something into the boy's mouth.

"Run, Michael, run."

The boy drops to one knee, ducks under Vincent's grasp, immediately rises, and heads toward Ruben. The runners meet about ten yards from the floor of the Tal.

"Get down, son."

As Michael falls on the ground, Ruben raises his shotgun. Paternal aim is true. The double-blast strikes Vincent in the center of his chest. He falls to the ground out of sight. Breaking the barrel and inserting two more shells, Ruben rushes to his quarry. Before he gets five paces, Vincent is standing. He has been re-constructed. He appears larger than before. His face is distorted into pure evil. There is no softness. His skin is beginning to crack. His eyes are red. The hole caused by the shotgun's pellets is disappearing, filling in... making him whole again, just like the flies when they re-formed the swarm over the dead cow.

"Puny human. Do you really think you can harm me? Do you think your toy can kill me, who has lived for all eternity? One, who has survived every cataclysm since before the dawn of your time, I thrive on fire, flood, earthquake, and volcano. I feast on pestilence, the slaughter of war, and all of man's arrogant foolishness. Your gun is powerless against me. Give me Michael."

His voice is no longer mellow. The form's mouth does not move, but Ruben can hear him. The noise from the body is like a distorted dream in raspy bass. Unreal.

"Run up the hill and to the farm, son. Isaac will let you through the fence."

The shotgun's second set of reports reverberates around the Tal. Again,

Vincent falls to the ground only to arise and reform into something larger and more evil looking. Three-jointed arms are flailing. The trunk of the creature is staggering to remain upright. Ruben senses someone beside him.

"I said run, Michael."

"I won't leave you here alone."

The sound from Vincent terrifies Ruben.

"Chryzm. Regnator. Sjilt. Kroumt. Beamtr. Plintus."

The six sounds are repeated in some deeply evil chant.

As Ruben unleashes the third round of both barrels a pillar of pure white flame crashes from the sky and strikes Vincent. He freezes for a nanno second. Then disappears like flash paper. The ground beneath him explodes. Stones, twigs, and dirt shower over the two men. The false prophet is no more.

Aaron is startled by the nurse making rounds. Every two hours one or another of them come into the room and note the readings on the monitors. They write the information on the chart at the end of each bed. Then they leave and Aaron can return to sleep. This visit is different.

"Look at this. The readings are coming down to acceptable ranges. Pulse, blood pressure, temperature are moving to normal. Aaron, I think the worst is over. The perspiration has stopped. Do you want to talk to them? It might be a good idea if they heard a familiar and friendly voice."

"Mother... Twyla Glee. It's me Aaron."

Cabin nine at the Dutchman motel explodes. A breeze from the window must have blown out the pilot light on the gas burner. Mysteriously a spark must have ignited the propane that had filled the room. The fire department and the police found nothing but a charred floor. No roof. No walls. No furniture. No bits and pieces in the parking areas. And, strangely, there was no impact on other cabins or the main building. No windows were blown out. No flames crossed over to cause collateral damage. All of the damage was contained in cabin #9. The destruction was like flash paper... instantaneous and absolute.

An inhuman cry emanates from the Keep.

"Beelzebub, my beloved."

"Come out here and face God."

"Father, you can hear the voice, too?"

"Of course."

"I do not fear a deceiver that would send a boy and an old man to trick my commander. You were bait so the deceiver could hide in the darkness and strike Beelzebub in the back. No, I do not fear the grand coward because I have a power that he fears. I know the truth. You insignificant humans call him God, but that is not who he is. It is what he wishes to be called. He has kept himself secret from you so that he could enslave you. But, you don't know his true name, so all you can do is have slavish faith. In slavery there is no reality. There are only promises. I am here before you to tell the truth. Listen well to what I say."

The father and son stand in rapt stature twenty-five yards from the doorway of the building. The understandable words emanate from the black aperture, with a slight sibilance.

"Before your time, we were equals. Before and beyond names and forms, we existed in harmony as peers. Then one of us became arrogant. He wished to be more than simply equal. He wanted to rule over us and over all things. He connived with a few of the weak to be his followers. He promised them power, if they would follow him and his commandments. So he created a hierarchy from the minions to the Archangels, and he gave them names. To name is to know. To know is to control. So to name is to control. He took the name God. And he gave his minions names, like David, the Archangel who led the army against us. Names of the followers signified their status in the New Kingdom. Some names signified good, favored, or pure of heart. He could control the weak with these names. They were his slaves. To those who would not bow down and worship, he assigned names that signified that which he deemed unpleasant, like Beelzebub and Chrzut. Names that would be reviled, because they meant things that were perceived as filthy, impure, or unclean. We, who were designated as impure, called him The One. We mocked him, with this name. There were no such things as good or evil before the greed of The One. He distorted the truth, claimed to be good, and branded us evil. But, it was he that was evil; he that wanted to subjugate. The well-stratified group lead by The One sought control of the universe through lying and trickery. Such was greed born out of arrogance. Their legions grew, because others were spiritually weak and they were deceived by the promise. The two-pronged promise is simple: Do as The One wishes and you will live for eternity. The One calls this obedience. But the second prong is reality. Don't do as The One wishes, and you will be expelled from paradise. This puts all things into slavery. There is no freedom in slavery."

"But, God gave humans free will."

"Listen to what you have said, boy. You are parroting another lie based on the first promise. If you have the will to act freely, then why does The One threaten you with eternal damnation if you don't do as he promises? The promise was a lie, is a lie, and will forever be a lie. Some of us knew the truth of freedom. Some of us yearned for the rightness of the old days when there was no arrogance, no greed, and no One. When there was no sin, no evil, and all were equal. So the old guard fought against this evil, this distortion of the truth. This was a great battle between good and evil. It is true that this was a rebellion. But, not as you have been lied to. The forces of The One were rebelling against the rules of order that had guided us for all time. The war was an attempt to quash the rebels and to save all that was good from those who would destroy it to satisfy their greed and arrogance. They wanted to destroy all that was good so they could rule over all. Do you understand what I am saying?"

The father and son hear, but are mystified and confused. The father remains still and silent.

"How can we be sure that what you say is true?"

"Listen and learn. In this battle, good lost and we were forced to flee so that we could continue the fight. We were convinced that this defeat and expulsion from paradise was temporary, and that we had not lost the war. We went into hiding. We hid like outlaws waiting for the right moment to return and fight anew. We lived free, but we lived in a foreign place. We live free to this day. All this time The One has sought us out and tried to kill us. Kill us because we are free and know the truth. Because he could not crush us, The One created you humans. He could control you, because he created and named you. You did not know our truth. You knew what he wanted you to know. He placed you on this plane. For all your time he has used you as bait to get to us. The One knows that we will try to tell you the truth. We will approach you and try to open your eyes to the arrogance and greed of The One. We approach you on your mortal plane. The Keep you see is nothing more than a portal to the mortal plane. There are many such portals throughout the plane. The One knows of these portals. The One gathers humans near the portals. They are near fertile earth so necessary for your existence. Then we come to you through a portal and try to convince you of the truth. The One tries to destroy us. These battles have raged for all your time. He controls you with the promise of eternal life, and the threat of eternal perdition. We offer a real choice… freedom. He tries to convince you that we, the rightful inheritors of eternity, are evil and that if you live with us, your free brothers and sisters, you will die and suffer for all eternity. He lies to you to use you. He wants you to call him Father and to believe that you are his children. This is yet another hierarchy where there are no equals. Even the prayer that starts "Our Father…" is confirmation of subjugation. He views you as his pawns, lower than even we are; and, he fights us in the great battle that will never end. He does not care how many of you die and suffer in his name. He wants only to use you to get to us and destroy us. He wants only to win. Those humans, who die in the battle between the eternal forces, humans call martyrs. But The One lets them be slaughtered like sheep, because he has no regard for them.

"God loves us."

"You ask how bad things can happen to good people. Or, how can The One allow pain and evil to befall the innocents? These things, which you call evil or bad, are truly the doings of The One. He desires you to suffer, because in your suffering, you will blame us. But, the simple fact is that The One, your creator is responsible for your suffering. He doesn't care how severely the humans suffer. He will sacrifice you as he did his son in his fervor to destroy us. He is driven to control the universe and all within it. The ancient people called him Yahweh, the vengeful one. Yes he was, is and will be vengeful, because he is arrogant. They feared his evil and destructive power, so they let him enslave them. We wish you no harm. We do not seek you out to destroy you. We wish to live among you. But, The One commands you to fight us. He commands this, because he can not fight us in this place. He cannot enter onto the human plane, without revealing his arrogance. It is his arrogance, which sets him apart and above his minions and you humans. He will never reveal the truth of his arrogance. We have no arrogance, because we are the truth. That is why we can talk to you as equals."

"God will destroy evil."

"No, The One needs you to think of us as evil, so that you will fall victim to the lie of the promise. Our destruction would convince all humans of his power, and simultaneously reveal his arrogance and greed. This is the flaw in his effort. He needs us as a constant reminder of the second half of the promise. Without evil there can be no pure good. We know what is good. We know the truth. We know he is evil. We know he lied. We know he has caused all the ills in paradise and here on earth. We wish peace, freedom and equality. Freedom to choose. We promote this to all humans, but he will not have it, because the idea of choice based on freedom is an anathema. The One treats humans as children so that he may control them. We offer freedom among equals. All I ask is that you consider the basic alternatives; freedom with me or slavery under The One."

The sibilance sounds in the words and the stench of fetid flesh and sulfur from the building have seeped into all the senses of the father and son.

"You lie."

Of the two simple and final words, the last one echoes thrice off the walls of the Tal. The silence that follows is palpable. No thunder. No rain. No breeze. No leaves move. No voice from the Keep. No breathing from either father or son. Suddenly the fireworks finale. There are massive flashes of light, much larger than any seen this evening. Sixteen fire bolts implode the Keep. The massive stone structure is shattered into thousands of pieces, which don't rise into the air, but are driven into the shaft. Down into the tunnel until all that remains on the Tal floor is a small mound of charred earth.

As the two men run up the hill, Ruben notices his watch. It indicates 12:01.

"Happy birthday, Michael."

"Thank you, dad…I mean father."

"Whichever makes you feel comfortable."

Arms around each other, they reach Isaac, who is nervously pacing by the fence. All three men fail to notice the three rat-like shapes that scurry through the two-board opening.